What's It Li[barcode]
In Love

Trese

FOLLOW ME

FACEBOOK: Trese McPherson

FACEBOOK READERS GROUP: Trese's Readers Spot

FACEBOOK AUTHOR'S PAGE: Author Trese

Acknowledgments

To my loyal readers: I would like to say thank you! Everything that could possibly go wrong with this book went wrong. STILL, y'all stuck it out with me in my reader groups, and believe it or not, it was y'all that got the job done.

Ladies of SDP: There are more of us now and the love is still the same only stronger. Thank y'all for pushing me and being understanding and dishing out that real ass advice that I only took in stride. I love all y'all crazy asses, and yes Shaundra that includes you, the main crazy one.

Mercedes G.: You know what it is. I don't know what you see in me, but I am and will always be forever grateful for it.

Mama, you my number one fan. Don't nobody go hard for me like you go hard for me! I love you more than I love your Cherry Cheesecake. (you know that's a lot)

My big sis Ki, you have been EVERYTHING! I cannot thank you enough!

Last but not least, to the Lord up above, who gave me this talent out of nowhere. To You be the glory. Thank You and Amen.

RECAP

Chandler

Where we left off…

It was already ten at night, and I was just now getting

dressed to go out with my girls. They had been blowing

my phone up, but I was too busy folding laundry to

answer. I had to make sure shit was good at home before

I went out to play.

I was listening to the radio and thinking about my

relationship with Hendrix, while I was getting the things I

needed for a bath. I sang for him last night. It may seem

like nothing, but that, for me, confirmed that Henny was

someone that I had really grown to love in this short period of time. I am in love with him. I know sometimes to him, I may seem distant, but it's not that. It's just that I know that if I was to fully put my guard down, I could become very clingy. No one wants a woman like that.

Me being distant is just me giving him his space. I don't want him to get tired of me and end up dumping me or worse, start spending his time elsewhere. I have waited years to be in a relationship that takes my mind on a journey and sends my heart above the clouds. Henny has been my heaven on earth and that's something that I don't want to let go. The hardest part has been learning how to be co-dependent on someone, which I never took an interest in until this morning.

Deciding to let down all barriers and let my man be a man, I shopped until I dropped and allowed him to pay for it all. Seeing how happy that made him made me reevaluate a lot of what I've been doing lately. I need to let Henny know that I know that he is the provider, the man of the house, and though I am his equal, I have no problem letting him lead and I follow.

My independency has become a mess. I won't even let Henny change a light bulb in the house. I'll go get the ladder and do it myself before I would ask him. I know he's noticed it, because I caught the look on his face when I made him put his dish back down. I don't ever want to see disappointment on his face again. I was going to tell, show, and prove to my baby that he is indeed needed more than he thinks he is. I depend on him a lot, especially for my happiness. He has managed to wake up a part of me that has been cold for so long. My heart is his, and there is no way that I'm letting go, so I gotta get my shit together.

I jumped in the tub and handled my business, not wanting to take up too much time soaking. I was out in thirty minutes, so I oiled my body down with this black butter that I got from the African store and put on a little makeup. I got dressed in a pair of hunter green, spandex, high-waist pants and put on my cream blazer, leaving it open with no bra. I was bold like that.

I took out my flexi rods and finger combed through the big curls that fell down my back and over my shoulders, with a part in the middle. I then donned my cream Gucci heels that Brailynn had bought me for graduation and put them bad boys on. I sprayed on a little of Mad About You, slapped on my diamond tennis bracelet and hoop earrings, grabbed my matching bag, and left out the house, pressed for time. It was now half past midnight.

I didn't make it very far. I apparently ran over something and ended up catching a flat. There was a gas station up ahead, but where I was parked on the side of the road had no lights and little to no traffic at all. I was scared as hell to get out of my vehicle. Shiddd, I've seen *Jeepers Creepers*. I reached to call Henny, for what seemed like, the thousandth time and got the same result, no answer. It kind of fucked with me, and it made me more worried about him than I was about myself, because

were like two hundred dollars. Do you know how many

pairs of shoes I can buy from DSW with that much? Or

how many sales I could hit at the Baby Gap or Children's

Place for my daughter. That shit got me worked all the

way up.

Right when I was about to go off on his ass, the

television screen that rested in my kidnappers' headrest

came on, and what I saw next had me worked up for a

whole new reason. On the small screen in front of me was

a video of Henny, straight fuckin' another girl in what

looked like someone's office. Though they were on the

couch, I could see the desk off on the side. The girl was

moaning loudly, while Henny hit it from the back,

unzipping her purple dress.

Tears ran from my eyes as I watched them fuck in numerous positions for an hour straight, until the screen went blue. I howled out in pain from feeling my heart break straight down the middle. Just when I thought that it was over, my attacker tortured me with more. Another video of Hendrix and the same girl fuckin' outside of someone's house on the front porch. The nigga didn't give a fuck who saw him! He wasn't trying to hide it!

I was in so much pain that I could hardly breathe. I started to hyperventilate and wheeze. It felt as if my throat was closing up. My abuser obviously wanted to just hurt me and not kill me, because he handed me a crumpled up brown paper sack that smelled just like beer. I didn't care though; I put it to my mouth and began breathing in and out slowly, catching my breath.

How could he do this? I let down my guard and gave him my heart! *Fuck!* I need him! At this point, I didn't even care what was going to happen to me now. I was no good after seeing the love of my life take life away from me. I felt numb, nonexistent… dead. The car came to a slow stop, and I was too fucked up to know, or maybe I didn't care that we were at my home. He parked the car and began to talk for the first time. I tried to catch his voice, but it was raspy like he had a bad cold.

"You know, Ma, this only happened because you are the only one in your circle that is connected to everyone in a strong way. I know it hurts, and I promise you it's going to get better, but you tell your best friend and that nigga of yours that payback is a bitch! And if I ain't happy, neither will they be."

With that, he got out of the car and opened the back door. I just knew he was about to kill me. I began fighting for the death of me, until he pulled his strap and began pistol whippin' me. I was no match for that. That was the moment that the love that I once had for Hendrix turned into hate. The moment I needed him most, he wasn't here because he was too busy out fuckin'. When the fuck boy grew tired, he looked down at my limp body and pulled the mask from his face. I couldn't believe the nigga that was standing in front of me with his gun drawn, pointing at my head.

"I'm sorry, Chandler."

"Zayden…" I got out before my world went completely black.

no harm to the eight-week-old fetus that was growing

inside of me. Yes, I was pregnant, and my home life was

in turmoil.

I wanted nothing to do with Hendrix if it wasn't

concerning our daughter, Breeland, or the baby that I was

carrying. Once I was released from this aggy ass hospital, I

had every intention of packing my daughter and myself up

and putting his cheating ass on a strict co-parenting

schedule.

"Chand, honey, please can you just talk to him? This

isn't just about you now; there are kids involved. You can

be mad all you want. Hell, you deserve to be upset with

him, but can't you do that after you inform the man about

his baby?" my mother, Renee, chastised me.

I almost rolled my eyes but forgot who I was in the presence of. I knew that she had no problem blacking my other eye, so I refrained from the urge.

"Where's my daddy?" I asked, instead, sounding like a spoiled brat.

Hendrix and my father Chao had yet to run into each other, and that, I was not prepared for. I knew that he and my brother, Chazman, wanted Hendrix's head, but on the strength of Breeland, I made them promise not to hurt him. Although he would deserve it, my love for him didn't want to see him hurt in the physical. I knew that my dad and Chaz both loved Breeland more than anything and would never want to see her upset or hurt, but by harming her dad, it would do just that.

"He will be here soon. I'm about to go out here and try to calm Henny down. Just so that you know, you're wrong for the shit that you're doing Chandler. I understand that you're mad and you're hurt, so you are running off of emotions, but baby, even if you don't forgive him, at least listen to what he has to say. You have been in this hospital for three days now, and he has yet to lay eyes on you. He doesn't know that you know about him stepping out on you. He doesn't even know who attacked you, and the most important of them all, he doesn't know about the baby that is growing inside of you.

I'm not going to keep stressing this to you, but you think about how it was for yourself and me when daddy wasn't there." she said, as she placed her opened hand on my flat tummy, careful not to put too much pressure on my ribs. My mother was ecstatic about our growing family. "The more grandchildren, the merrier," were her exact words. She gathered her things and left me alone with my thoughts.

I sat in silence as I looked around the stark white room. It was filled with all kinds of flowers, stuffed animals, and balloons. I didn't know where half of the gifts came from, and to be quite frank, I didn't really care. I closed my eyes as I listened to nothing. Just the sounds of different monitors beeping letting me know that I was still alive even though I felt dead to the world.

Images of Hendrix and I began to play over and over in my head. I hated when that happened. It was only when I was alone did I sit and think about every touch whatever I am feeling is pushed to the back of my mind to ensure that her every need is met. I never want my daughter to see me broken and hurt over no man… not even her father. I don't want her to grow up thinking that it was okay to be weak for a man even if I was at the moment.

Knock Knock.

The light tapping at my door had me quickly drying my tears. I ran my hands through my hair trying to bring order to my appearance. I assumed that it was the nurse, because I specifically asked for no guests while I was here.

Seconds later, the door swung open and in walked Brailynn, Rorilynn and ZaNoni. They all held irritated looks on their faces, and I knew that I was in deep shit with the three of them. Since I had been in the hospital, I had been refusing their visits. Mainly because I wasn't ready to discuss the details of the other night. My girls didn't know who attacked me, about Henny cheating, or about the baby I was carrying. No one knew anything besides my dad, mom, and brother. I didn't want my girls' sympathy, and I didn't want to upset Brailynn. I knew that, without a doubt, she was going to be pissed with her brother and ex-boyfriend indefinitely.

I raised up in my bed and sat silently while I watched them take seats around the room. Once they were situated, we sat looking at one another as the tension in the room built thick.

"You need to start talking… open your mouth and don't close it until we know everything." Rori said, giving me her no bullshit glare. I hated how assertive she could be, but I knew that it was all in good stride. I was a weak

spot for Rori, and I was starting to feel bad for avoiding

them all this time. We were better than that. I took a deep

breath before I began to talk.

"Zayden did the attack." I spoke softly.

My eyes focused on Brailynn, and I watched her

emotions play out on her face. From shock, to hurt, to

anger, and they had all taken over as she shot out of her

chair, merely throwing it across the room. She rushed

towards my bedside and fell into my arms crying harder

than I've seen her cry in a minute. I said nothing and held

her as she sorted through her feelings. Once she had

gotten her tears under control, she then sat up, still in my

bed with her nostrils flaring.

"I'm killing that bitch!" she seethed through clenched teeth and a locked jaw. I looked to the other two and watched as Rori pinched the bridge of her nose only to release it and pinch it again. Her face was red and damp from the tears that were cascading down her beautiful face. I focused my attention on Noni and already knew that she was planning the next contents of her special black bag, as she paced back and forth speaking lowly in Spanish. She almost looked possessed, and I was starting to consider calling the chaplain in here to perform an exorcist if need be. I've learned over the years that a Spanish temper is one that you don't want to play with.

"What else..." Rori asked, calmly. Almost too calm for my liking. I didn't want to keep going after laying something so thick on them. Zay once meant something

"Brai! Get the fuck off!" he gritted, as he tried his best to block my hits and hold my hands. I was so mad and hurt that I was emotionally fighting, therefore my strength was ten times as much as it would have been.

"Yasss bitch! That's right! Whoop his ass, Gutta B!" I heard Noni in the background hyping me up like we were fighting one of these hoes out on the streets. "Work his ass, Brai! Uppercut that nigga!" she continued, and if I wasn't so into what I was doing, then I would have fell out laughing at her ass.

Suddenly, I could feel myself being lifted up in the air causing me to lose my grip on Henny's shirt. It was then that I began to kick to get the job done. Landing my feet in his chest and ribs.

"How the fuck could you!?" I yelled with tears burning in the corners of my eyes. "Huh, how could you hurt her like that? How could you cheat on her; she took in your daughter!" I cried at the severity of the situation.

Chandler was too good of a woman for what my brother did to her. There was no excuse that he could come up with other than that he was a sorry ass nigga that didn't deserve her. I looked at Henny, as he looked at me with an ashen face as if he had seen a ghost.

"Cheated, I didn't—," he started to lie, but I shut that shit down still being held in the air by I don't know who.

"Shut the fuck up lying to me! Zayden attacked her and laid out all your dirty laundry in the process! He got you on video fuckin' Temperra the night of the attack!" I shouted, breaking free of whoever's hold and clocking

Henny one good time in the eye. I was praying that it was

going to swell up and resemble my sister's.

This time, when I was lifted into the air and was

positioned against the wall, I was placed in handcuffs.

Before the officer could even read me my Miranda rights,

my crazy boyfriend came rushing towards us with his face

showing his displeasure. Chazman was on some good

bullshit, today. I could see it in his eyes.

"Get your pig ass the fuck back. I got her!" he yelled,

as he snatched the keys out of the officer's hand so that he

could uncuff me. In the process, another scrawny officer

showed up and tried to detain Chaz. "Yo, dawg, you better

back the fuck up, yo. Let me get my girl then we out."

Chazman said, as he finally got the cuffs off and pulled me

into his arms. I immediately felt at ease, falling into his embrace. He looked up and locked eyes with Henny, then threw him a look that could kill. Henny squared up ready to tag with Chaz.

"Let's go; didn't neither one of us come here for this stupid shit." I said, tugging on Chaz's hand, as I made way towards the entrance of the building. If we stayed another minute longer, I knew that it was bound to be a blood bath. By then, the backup that these scary ass policemen had called would be here, and jail definitely wasn't the place for a 'G' like me.

"I'm out of here. I am with child, and I will not let Satan's spawn have his way with my delicate soul." Noni spat, glaring at Henny. "Brai, I'll see you later. We need to talk about that situation." she said in a softer tone. I knew

overload. I cried my heart out thinking of my best friend. *Why would they do this to her of all people?*

"Are you pregnant? How can you just cry on the spot like that?" he countered with the biggest most goofiest grin on his face. Watching him watch me and not the road, I couldn't help but laugh at him.

"Chazman, you know my body better than I do. You know I'm not pregnant. In fact, my period is due in--,"

"Three days, I know." he sighed, heavily, cutting me off. I smiled inwardly at how he was so in-tune with my body. Chaz knew things about me that I didn't even know about myself. Our connection was like two strong forces that couldn't help but to collide and make this big, purple, magnetic energy that anyone could feel when we were around.

"Just, think about having my baby, okay? Can you do that for me?" he asked, leaning over and grabbing my hand he began to place soft kisses on the back of it. Looking into his face, I knew that there was nothing in the world that I wouldn't do for him. I was just so afraid of having a baby and being someone's mother. I could see myself failing at it miserably. My mother passed before she could teach me anything valuable of that nature. All the lessons that I had been taught, such as, the birds and the bees talk, personal hygiene, and love, all came from Hendrix, Mama Nae, and experience. "Please, just give me your eggs, Ma." I couldn't help but laugh at Chaz's ass. I looked over at him, and the fact that he held a serious look on his face had me laughing even harder.

"I'll think about it baby; I promise." I said still laughing. I leaned over and kissed his lips, and we continued our drive to his house in a comfortable silence.

I sat back in seat and allowed my thoughts to shift to Zayden. I felt myself getting hot all over again. Chaz must have sensed it, because he reached over and gave my hand a firm squeeze, then brought it to his lips for a series of feather-light kisses, which always calmed me down.

"I want in." I said, referring to whatever he and Chao had planned for Zay. Never to speak detail in the car, I kept it short and simple, but he knew what I was talking about.

Chaz stopped his trail of kisses and looked to me, I guess to see if I was serious or not. I was, and once he realized that, he started back raining kisses on the back of my hand, fingers, wrist, and forearm.

"Cool." he spoke after a while. Satisfied, I reclined my seat back and allowed all the horrific shit that I wanted to do to Zay to take me to a much-welcomed high. I couldn't wait to play the grim reaper and take his pathetic little life, just like he tried to take mine, because if he would have killed Chand, then that's exactly what it would have been in equivalence to.

~~~~~~~~

"Brai!" I heard my name being called, but I couldn't force myself to look into the light. I was laying down taking a nap before it was time to go meet up with ZaNoni so that we could have lunch before going back up to visit Chand. I hated the way that I had stormed out of her room earlier, but I couldn't stomach to face her at the moment knowing

that two people who were tied to me hurt her in such a

fucked up way. I had to see her, hug her, and apologize for

the way that I acted earlier.

I felt someone sticking what felt like a feather in my

ear tickling me. I swatted it away, and not even a second

later, the same feeling came to my nose. Swatting the

person away again, I turned over and huffed out my

frustrations.

Minutes had passed, and I was just getting ready to

start snoring when I felt light nudges on my arm. I knew

then who it was trying to get my attention. I opened my

eyes, and a pair of tight, slanted, dark brown ones were

staring back at me with a goofy grin on his face.

"What are you doing here? I thought you were going over to your mother's house." I said, as I sat up in the bed and wrapped my arms around Lil' Chaz. In the almost year that I had been dating Chazman, he and I had grown super close. Like, he-was-my-own-child close. I loved Chazman so much that I had no problems loving his child, and his child seemed to have no problems loving me.

"Cum on now. You know I only went because I had to go. If it was my choice, I would live with you and my daddy full-time." he said, as he kicked off his Jordan's that I had gotten him the week before, and made me scoot over. He picked up the remote and started flipping through the channels. I sat and watched him as he crossed his feet and threw his arm behind his head as he settled on a basketball game. The kid was so much like Chazman that it was scary.

"My daddy told me that you were going to go up to the hospital so that you could visit with my auntie. Can you cook before you go?"

See what I mean? He was Big Chaz through and through. I chuckled and rubbed my fingers through his curly hair and kissed his cheek. He looked at me with that same goofy grin and adoration in his eyes as he always did, and I'm sure mine mirrored.

I got out of the bed and slipped on my house shoes before going into the bathroom to freshen up. When I got out, I went into my closet, and threw on a powder gray Nike sweat suit along with my neon green, gray, and black Air Max 95's. I left my deep burgundy red hair hanging down and threw on a pair of silver hoops. I looked at

myself in the mirror and almost pissed my pants when I

saw Chazman standing behind me in the reflection. I didn't

hear him walk up, so he scared me shitless.

"I'm hungry. Can you cook before you go?" he

asked, sounding just like his son.

"Dude, you almost just gave me a freaking heart

attack!" I said, trying to regulate my breathing.

"Oh my God, Becky, I am so freaking sorry!" he

said, in a very proper and high-pitched voice with his palms

flat against both of his cheeks. *This nigga!* I laughed while

shaking my head and playfully hitting him on his chest, as I

moved passed him to make my way downstairs to the

kitchen to prepare them something quick to eat before I

go. I settled on fried chicken, because it was Lil Chaz's

favorite, macaroni and cheese, because that was Big Chaz's, and cabbage, because I made sure they both always had something green to eat.

The whole time I cooked, Chazman sat in the kitchen and watched me. I could tell that he had something he wanted to say but was waiting until I fixed his plate to do so.

"What is it, Chazman?" I asked, after I sat his hefty-sized plate of food in front of him and called Lil' Chaz down to eat.

"I want you to have my baby." he said, flat out, as if it was nothing.

I rolled my eyes not ready to have this conversation again. I had just agreed with him to think about it a few hours ago, but I should have known that that wasn't good enough for him. I picked up my purse and let out a shaky breath. I was going to have to voice my fear to Chaz sooner or later if I wanted to get this topic off of my back.

I knew he wouldn't be happy, but he would understand, nonetheless. That was one thing that I loved about Chazman. He voiced his feelings without a problem, and he wasn't opposed to me having an opinion either. We could agree to disagree all day every day, but he still went to sleep and woke up loving me, and that was all that mattered to me.

"That's alright. You gone make me trap your ass." he mumbled, with frustration, as he dug into his food.

I threw my purse over my shoulder and walked over to my big baby, then kissed the corner of his mouth.

Chapter 3. Hendrix

Last night, we had an argument

You told me you love me

All the things that I said, I never meant, no baby

I didn't mean to make you cry, I didn't mean to make you say

bye, bye, bye

I was outside of the hospital sitting in my car,

smoking on some good 'Dro and licking my wounds. I had

Silks song "Lose Control" on repeat because them niggas

was speaking exactly how I was feeling. Shit was all crazy, and I was all fucked up right now. Things in my life were completely falling apart. I hadn't been the same since I woke up three days ago at the sounds of Brailynn's screams on the other end of my phone. When she told me about Chandler's attack, I immediately jumped out of bed only to then realize that I wasn't even at my house.

When I looked around at my surroundings, then towards the bed that I was just in, I could have died when I saw my jump-off Temperra sleeping soundly. I had never felt so low in my life than I did at that moment. While I was laid up with that slow ass trick, my fuckin' wife was being beaten. *How could I have been so fuckin stupid?* Now, Chand doesn't even want to have anything to do with me.

At first, I thought that it was because she didn't want me to see her bruised and battered. That was, until Brailynn let it be known that she was onto me and knew about my infidelity. Then, to top all of that off, my nigga Zay was behind all of this shit. I couldn't believe how quick my best friend turned into a foe. Everything was everything, though. Zay knew just like everyone else did that he was on borrowed time. Wasn't no way in hell that I was going to allow him to get away with this bullshit.

I finished up my blunt and went to sit outside of the hospital on the curb to get some fresh air. I couldn't believe the shit that I was going through. Yeah, I cheated, but I never thought that it would come back on me like this. A nigga was out here sick for real.

I thought about my next move as far as Chand and I went. Just the thought of her knowing about me giving her dick away had me feeling sick to my stomach. I pictured what a hurt expression would look like on her face, and I couldn't take it. I leaned over and emptied my stomach, which consisted of nothing but fluids, because I hadn't had an appetite in days. I was fucked up out here. All I knew was that I needed my girl, and I wasn't letting her go for nothing. We were just going to have to work through this. That was really the only option she had.

"Hey, come talk to me." I looked up at the familiar voice and saw Mama Nae standing over me. She handed me napkins and a water bottle, so that I could rinse my mouth out and get myself together. Her presence was making me feel even shittier, because I knew I had fucked

was still as devastated as I was when I found out just how bad shit really was. Nevertheless, I had one of the most important people in Chand's life on my team, and I was going to definitely use this to my advantage. Moving on to more pressing matters, I spoke about what really needed to be addressed as Chandler's protector.

"I'm killing him," I said, referring to Zay. I didn't have to say no more than that. I'm positive Mama Nae knew who I was talking about. Zay's bitch ass was out of here, and there was nothing else to it.

"Get in line, Son," she chuckled and patted my back, giving me some much-needed comfort. "Chao and Chaz are already on it." I tensed up hearing their names, because I knew that there was a major problem between us now. If I blamed myself, then I already know that they did as well.

Even though I fucked up, I was a man before anything, therefore if they came to me on some bullshit, then I was going to give them what they were asking for with no hesitations.

"They're upset, but they will get over it. Chandler is grown, so whatever she decides to do, we have no choice but to respect and accept it."

My mind went on a pause break when Mama Nae spoke. She always knew what I was thinking or feeling without me opening my mouth and saying a word. I remained quiet, because I really didn't know what to say. No words could describe how I was feeling at the moment. I just needed to see my baby.

"I gotta wrap with her for real; she ain't trying to see me or hear shit that I gotta say."

"You know how stubborn Chandler can be when it comes to her feelings, but I agree that the two of you need to talk sooner rather than later, because even if she doesn't take you back, there are kids involved." she said, as she stood up.

I caught on to the mention of her saying kids with an "s" meaning more than one, and it made my heart swell. If Chandler was pregnant, then I'm most definitely not letting her go now. Right when I was about to ask Mama Nae about it, I was cut off by my baby girl screaming my name and running up to me. I swept down and picked Breeland up, then held her tight. At this point, all I seemed to have was her. I fucked up with Chandler, and now everyone hates me.

"Are you here to see my mommy, too?" she asked, with her arms still wrapped around me. I placed her back on her feet, but before I could answer her, I heard Chao's loud voice booming in the near distance.

"WHY THE FUCK IS HE HERE!?" he yelled, before he charged at me, sending a barrage of blows my way. I wasted no time defending myself and swinging back. We were outside of the hospital fighting like we were in the middle of a boxing ring going round for round. For every bone-crushing blow that he sent, I made sure that I countered back with my own. I hated to be fighting my father-n-law, but fuck it. It was what it was.

"Daddy! Pots!" The sound of Breeland calling our names brought the both of us to an immediate halt. The terrified look on her face had me wanting to kick my own ass. I just couldn't get shit right; it's like I was messing up all around.

"Baby girl, Daddy's sorry, ok?" I picked her up, and she began to cry uncontrollably. My heart broke with each sob that left her mouth.

"Come on; you need to get cleaned up and go talk to your woman. This shit cannot go on! While y'all are fighting each other, where the hell is Zay, and why the fuck is he still breathing!?" Mama Nae yelled, as she took Breeland out of my arms and handed her to Chao. "Take her to the house, now Chao, and don't fix your mouth to say shit to me." she said through clenched teeth.

Chao dropped his head in shame, grabbed a still weeping Breeland, and left. I knew that he was in deep shit with Mama Nae, and that he was regretting his actions in front of Bree just as much as I was. Mama Nae turned and glared at me long and hard before she spoke.

"Get your words together and let's go!" she said, and turned on her heels, not giving me much of a choice but to follow.

We went inside of the hospital where I slipped into the restroom to clean my face free of the blood that was leaking from my lip and nose. Between Chao and Brai, I knew that I was going to have to ice my wounds to keep them from swelling. I shook my head at all the bullshit that was taking place today. *This shit has got to get better.*

When I came out from the restroom, Mama Nae was right there to lead the way up to Chandler's room since I was on the none visitor's list. I followed behind her onto the elevators, up to the tenth floor, and down the long, white, private hallway that led to Chandler's room. With each step that I took, I became more and more nervous. I didn't know what she was going to say or do at this point, and after the day's events, I wasn't prepared. Right when we got in front of Chand's room door, Mama Nae stopped then turned to face me.

"Remember what I said; she's stubborn, and you messed up, so take whatever she throws at you on the chin. I believe the two of you can get through this. I know what real love looks like, and I see it in your eyes when you look at my baby. It's the same look I see in her father's eyes every time he looks at me. Do whatever it is that you have to do Hendrix, and promise me that you will fix it. She needs you… now more than ever." she said, as she pulled me in close and gave me a hug that only a mother could. I watched as she walked back down the hall and stepped onto the elevators. The last words that she spoke rang in my ear on repeat, as I thought on them being true or not. *Does she really need me?*

I stood outside of the room door and just thought for a minute. I didn't know what I was walking into. This would be my first time laying eyes on my baby since the morning that all of this shit had gone down. She was dealing with everybody but me, but all of that was about to change.

Without knocking, I went into the room unnoticed and saw her snuggled up with Rori at the head of her bed, while Brai and Nons were at the foot. They had pizza, magazines, and iPads and shit all scattered about the bed. Soft music was playing in the background, and I caught

y'all can come back." I spat, looking directly at the three

mustytears so that they knew that I wasn't for any shit. Rori

looked to Chand, and Chand gave her a slight nod of

approval. They all climbed off the bed, slipped on their

shoes, and exited out the room, one by one all rolling their

eyes at me. Rori, on the other hand, bumped into me on

purpose, trying her hardest to knock my arm off my body.

I had suspected that she would do some shit like that, and I

could bet money that she wanted to lay hands on me just

like Brailynn did. *Fuckin' females, yo.*

Getting straight to the point, I spoke what I felt

needed to be said. It was time that I laid my heart out on

the table. My cards were shown, and my heart was dangling

from my sleeve. I was weak in this moment, and as long as

it warranted me my girl's presence, I didn't give the slightest fuck.

"I'm sorry. That's the first thing that I am going to say, because it's true. I cheated on you because I was selfish. I didn't consider your feelings and was only looking out for mine." I took a deep breath fighting my emotions and continued.

"I needed you, Chand. I needed you in the worst way, and sometimes, most times I felt that you didn't feel the same way. You never came to me for anything. Not even for the simple shit. It had gotten to the point where I was beginning to feel like less of a man." I said, shaking my head.

I hated how I was explaining myself. The words weren't coming out right, and I was sounding more and more like a bitch with each passing second. "Just please try to understand that that hoe… them hoes, don't mean nothing to me. It was an ego thing and that was it. I can't express how sorry I am, baby. I hate me right now for hurting you. That was the last thing that I wanted to do. All I ask is that you try, try your best to not give up on me…"

My voice trailed off, because like I said earlier, I really didn't know what to say. Everything I said was the truth, but how do you really apologize for hurting someone so badly. Seeing the look on Chandler's face was enough to make a grown man cry. I used to see so much love, respect, and admiration in her eyes when she looked at me. Now, all I see is nothing. Not even hatred.

"Honestly, fam, I appreciate you for stopping by…"

Fam? I thought. "But what we had is now over with. If it's not concerning my daughter, then we have absolutely nothing to talk about." she said, as she laid back on her bed and got comfortable, as if she was dismissing me of my presence. "Once I leave here, I'll be by to pick up my Bree. She'll be staying with me at my place, and you and I can sit down then and come up with a co-parenting schedule." she said, pissing me the fuck off.

"Look, I understand that you're mad and all, but you ain't leaving, and you damn sure ain't splitting our family up!" I yelled, almost reaching the peak of my frustrations. Chandler was trying the fuck out of me with this shit.

"Hendrix, just go. You heard what I said. Whether I take her or not, your family will still be split." she snapped,

chirping, and Chandler's hospital room was completely

empty. *Damn!*

"She really left me."

Chapter 4. Chazman

"Man, where the hell is this bitch." I mumbled under my breath. I was growing more and more irritated as the seconds ticked by. Chen and I were sitting outside of Butterfly's mother's raggedy ass house waiting on Zay's bitch ass to come out so that we could snatch him up. It took us little to no time to find him. Once we put word out to the Mafia, we had the exact location and eyes on him the following morning. With him being such a wanted man, one would think that he would hide out somewhere else, but nah. He ran straight into the mouse's trap, so finding this motherfucka was easy.

I felt my phone vibrate in my pocket and pulled it out. Seeing that it was my baby, I was anxious to see her reply to the message that I had sent her earlier.

Baby Girl: *Chazman, can we talk bout this later? I'm at work.*

I sighed reading her reply. Everything between Brai and I was perfect except for when it came to this shit. I started tapping my screen hard as hell as I replied to her message, taking my anger out on my phone.

Me: *I don't give a fuck if you were on the moon. All ur friends bout to be poppin kids out and u tryna wait 4 wat?*

I'm bout to be 30, Ma. I ain't got nothin but a couple of good

nuts left in me.

This shit with Brai's ass was only adding to my

frustrations. Here we sat in someone else's hood all the way

out in Philly, and I was hungry, out of herb, and quite

frankly, tired of going back and forth arguing with Brailynn

through text messages because she won't give me a baby.

To add to it, Lil Chaz's mother, Jamiee, won't stop calling

my fuckin' phone. I swear, I hated the day I met and

fucked that bitch. Since then, my life has been like a horror

movie, constantly being chased by a crazed baby mama.

This girl just wouldn't give up. I done had restraining

orders put against her and everything, but there wasn't no

stopping her.

Jamiee was a one-night-stand that resulted in a baby. After I learned that she was pregnant, I admit that I would still sleep with her every now and then, but I made my intentions clear that I didn't want a relationship, and that she was nothing more to me than my baby mother. She seemed to understand that all the way up until the day she came home from the hospital after giving birth to Lil' Chaz. The plan was for her to stay at her house, and I would come over and help out every day, on top of her having a nanny, so that she could still do the hood rat shit that she liked to do. But boy didn't I get a surprise one night after I came in from the club drunk as hell and walked into my bedroom ready to crash and sleep my liquor off.

It shocked me to see her crazy ass in my room, on my bed with a fussy baby and shitty diapers and rags soaked in baby vomit on my Versace covers. When I asked her ass how she got in, she said that I gave her a key. Knowing damn well that I didn't, we got into a huge fight that turned physical. I had whooped her ass before I knew it, but that seemed to only make her ass more possessed.

Throughout the years of raising Lil Chaz, it had been nothing but hell dealing with her. She had turned every woman that had entered my life away. It had gotten to the point that I was afraid to even admit that I was involved with someone for the fear of what Jamiee would do to them. She didn't mind, fighting, cutting, or doing anything to make a woman look at me as too much baggage. In her mind, she thought that when it came time for me to settle down that I would choose her, but like I've told her so many times, "Baby girl, if you ain't the one, you just ain't the one."

I was jarred from my thoughts when Chen's heavy-handed ass began to pat on my chest repeatedly to gain my attention.

"There that fucker go right there!" he spoke with urgency, as I sat up in my seat and peered towards the front of the house. True enough, there Zay was coming out of the house like shit was all fine and dandy. The fact that he seemed unfazed like the Mafia wasn't at his head pissed me off.

I reached behind my seat and grabbed my weapon of choice. Chen and I hopped out of my truck, which was parked directly behind Butterfly's old Toyota Corolla.

Before Zay could even reach the handle, I popped out of nowhere like a piece of toast fresh out of a toaster and went upside his head with the tire jack just like he did my sister. I came down on his ass repeatedly until he dropped to the ground. He was laid out on the concrete with his back arched and his mouth wide open, with no sound coming out. Dumb ass was in so much pain that he couldn't scream or move. It was midday, and I was beating his ass outside his in-law's house, not giving one fuck about who saw me.

"That's enough; you are going to kill him before we can get back to the port." Chen said, stopping me from having my fun. I snatched Zay's flimsy body up and threw him over my shoulder, while Chen held the trunk open for me. I threw his ass in the trunk by his legs first, leaving his head out by accident. Chen ended up closing the hood down hard on his neck damn near taking the man's head off.

"Decapitate his ass then Uncle Chen," I laughed, getting a kick out of the deep gash that was placed on the side of Zay's neck.

"You set that up. Why would you place him in the trunk legs first?" he chuckled, as he sat up against the trunk of the car and lit up a cigarette. I wasn't a tobacco smoker, so watching him take his edge off only made me more irritated than I was before.

"Come on, so that we can get this shit over with." I sighed, heading for the driver's side door. I slid in, cranked the car up, then pulled into traffic as if nothing was wrong. Because shit, there wasn't. I was part of the Chinese Mafia, and that was a requirement. You learn how to snatch and bag a nigga at the age of seven.

It's my baby mama (yeenknow) I want child support

She get welfare checks, but I stay in court

It's my baby mama (yeenknow) she be ridin' Cady

And she always lookin' for sugar daddies

When the Three 6 Mafia's ringtone began to play, it took everything in me not to chunk my phone out of the window. Deciding to answer and put her ass in her place for the fifth time today, I tapped the green button.

"The fuck you want, Jamiee?" I gritted, already ready to hang up. *God, I hate this bitch.*

"Uhh, where you at? I need some money. Lil Chaz needs some shoes." she said with her ghetto ass. I could

She'll buy Lil Chaz a fit and some kicks before she buy herself something. She goes above and beyond for him. That's why I love her the way I do. I hadn't ever loved a woman outside of my moms and baby sis. Brailynn came in like a thief in the night and robbed ya boy for every ounce of feelings he's got. That girl was my everything, straight up.

"Yo, Jamiee and Brai must have never ran into one another?" Chen asked. I had the dumb broad on speaker so he heard everything that was said between Jamiee and me. I wasn't about to wrap my shit up trying to drive and talk to her silly ass at the same time.

"You see she still living, ain't it? That should be your answer right there. Brailynn ain't got a problem with canceling a bitch. She goes hard for hers." I boasted, proud that I got a girl who loves me just as much as I love her. We were straight insane about each other, and that was exactly how it should be.

"Jamiee better be careful. I saw with my own two eyes how Brai can get down. That night at the club, she whooped ole girl so fast with that champagne bottle that I just knew the bitch was kissing death." he laughed. I just shook my head. My baby did have a temper, but she's getting better at handling it. This dick I was giving her left her not having a care in the world. That's just the way I liked her too; stress-free.

Back in China Town, I pulled into the underground tunnel that led to the torture chamber where we would be holding Zay at. I had a nice little room set up that I thought ould be perfect for him until the following Sunday when he was scheduled to perish.

"Help me prep this nigga." I said, as I grabbed the paper brown sack out of the back seat and climbed out of the car. Chen opened the trunk, and I couldn't help but laugh at the fear that this big burly ass nigga had in his eyes. To be quite frank, there was no way in hell that I should've been able to take him down by myself. His big ass could have easily taken over that scruff.

"Here, lock his bitch ass up." I said, handing Chen the zip ties to cuff Zay's hands while I took a couple pair to restrain his feet.

"Listen, I've been down with Henny since I've met him--," he was saying before Chen elbowed him so hard in his mouth that a tooth went down his throat and left him looking like Danny Brown.

"Damn, Daniel!" I said, as I fell over laughing. I swear, I crack myself up.

"Muthafuck Henny! You put your hands on my Goddaughter. Big fuckin no *no.*" I sat back, watching as Chen laid hands on this fool. It brought back pleasant memories of him and my pops putting in work when I was a youngin. They hardly ever got their hands dirty now.

"Aight, that's enough. We ain't got no oxygen tank out here if your old ass pass out." I cracked patting Chen on his back.

"Help me get this fucker in the room," Chen said all out of breath. I couldn't help but laugh. His Chinese ass was sweating through the all black suit he had on making him look like a killer whale.

I assisted in helping the bitch over Chen's shoulder and led the way up a flight of stairs that led to the entrance of our underworld. Straight beyond the door was pitch black; the only light that could be seen was coming from the little space between the floor and the door that was all the way at the end of the hall.

Using that as my guide, we made our way to the door and I opened it using the single key that went to every room in the building. Pushing the door open, the light immediately blinded me from being in the darkened hall. I was seeing blue circles and all kinds of other weird shit every time that I blinked my eyes. Getting a better focus, I saw that not much had changed since last week when I was here.

When you first walked beyond the steel door, the first room was set up like a hospital's operating room. This was where I would come if I was to get popped. Bypassing all of that into the second room were four electric chairs posted in every corner. This was for Mafia members who have crossed us. Their fate was always the electric chair. We never torture family. Walking to the door that was just beyond that room, I paused for Chen to catch up. He was having a hard time toting Zay. I looked back at him and cracked the hell up laughing.

"Step back. You don't want something to pop out and getcha," I said, once he was standing beside me. I twisted the doorknob and pushed the door open.

Sssss. Sssss.

"Aaahh!" I heard a loud screeching girly scream followed by a loud thud. I turned my head to see that Zay was now on the floor, and Chen was looking at me like he had suffered a heart attack.

"Nigga, was that you?" I asked him not being able to hold my laugh.

"I swear, this tops all the crazy shit that you have ever done. You filled the room with live snakes, yo!" Chen freaked. I forgot that this is one of his biggest fears.

"My bad man, come on; just help me get him in the chair and tied down." I said, as I proceeded through the room.

"You out of your fuckin mind; take your ass on in there. I'll be here when you get out." he huffed, as he pulled out yet another cigarette and lit it. Ready to get the shit over with, I picked up Zay, who was damn near passed out and walked into the room that was filled with thirteen hundred snakes. They were all nonpoisonous, because we needed him to be alive for what we had planned on his final day. However, there were quite a few Boa's in here that could probably swallow him whole if they got hungry enough.

I placed him into the chair and secured his wrist to each handle of the chair using the metal cuffs that were attached. I then did the same thing to his feet making sure that each ankle was secure to the legs of the chair.

"Hurry up! This shit is making my flesh crawl!" Chen called out. I shook my head at him. I really did need a right-hand-man that didn't mind getting down and dirty. Chen had phobias out of the ass, and my pops was just simply getting old.

I walked out of the room and locked the door behind me. We then headed out of the warehouse and took the long dark hall back out to the car.

"How the fuck did you come up with that shit?" I looked at Chen, as he rubbed his fat, sweaty palms on his pants suit. His hair was drenched with sweat, as he continued looking over his body.

"Oh shit, Chen! You brought one with you!" I faked panicked. His ass almost jumped clean through the windshield trying to get out of the car. I was laughing so

hard that my head and stomach began to ache.

"Fuck you! I'm retiring! I'm not about to keep

working with your childish ass." The fact that he was so

upset had me laughing even harder. He got back into the

car, and I put it in drive and headed through to the other

end of the tunnel. Coming out, we were on the other side

of town, almost forty-five minutes from my house, where

Chen's car was parked. Finally calming down enough from

my laughter, I answered his question.

"Zay's a snake so he might as well live with them." I

said, closing the topic. I was ready to be rid of this nigga, so

that I could get back to my regular scheduled

programming.

Chapter 5. Rorilynn

"Okay, this house is listed for 9.9 million. It was built from the ground up making you guys its very first owners. With a check today, I can have your keys by tomorrow evening." I stood in the middle of the spacious living area thinking about what in God's good name I could possibly do with the place.

Moriah and I had been out home shopping for the past few weeks now, and this was the best that we've seen so far that the real estate agent, Mo, and I had agreed upon.

"What do you think, Mrs. B? This is your show; whatever you want, baby. You know that it's yours." Mo said, as he walked up behind me and wrapped his hands around my waist. I melted in his arms, blushing at how, after months of being together, he's still everything that I could ever want in a man.

I looked up at the agent and caught her staring with an envious look on her face. Jackie worked for Mo as his personal assistant slash publicist, and anything else that required her to be in his presence. I disliked that bitch. A blind man could tell that she wanted my man. What she failed to realize, though, is that I was in love with Moriah and had not a problem jacking Jackie the fuck up over him.

I was new to this 'love and having feelings' shit. This was my first time being in a relationship, so on top of my already craziness, being in love has made me crazier, and I was totally okay with that. Giving that bitch a knowing smirk, I turned in my baby's arms and kissed him deeply.

"I think this is the one. I love it, baby!" I crooned, not putting on a show anymore, because it was true. I actually did love this house. Seven bedrooms, nine baths, indoor and outdoor pool, acres of land, basketball court, horse stable, and a clear blue water pond with the most prettiest fish swimming around in it. I was truly in awe of the place and couldn't wait to sign my name on the dotted line.

"Jackie, you heard my baby. She wants it. Get the paperwork together for me as soon as you can so that we can sign." Mo told her, all while looking into my eyes smiling like he had just struck gold.

"Very well then," that hoe Jackie said smugly. "I'll make the call now and give you two a minute." she said dismissing herself, which was good for her, because I was about to do it… permanently. She knew like I did that, whatever I said, goes. One word to Moriah, and she would be out of there. Seeing as though I was secure in myself, and I believed with everything in me that Mo wouldn't do anything to intentionally hurt my feelings, I looked over a lot of shit that she did, because I knew that wasn't shit happening her way.

"Baby," I looked up at Mo looking down at me and could see the nervousness in his eyes just as I heard the plea in his voice. I started to slick panic, and my mind ran rapidly with what it was that he had to tell me that made him scared to just spit it out. I got my answer when Moriah

got down on one knee before me.

"Rorilynn, Ma, look at you. When we first met, I told

you that you would be mine and here we are. Not only do

you belong to me, but I to you. I have never thought about

marriage until I saw your beautiful, hazel eyes, banging ass

body, and long, nappy ass hair," he said laughing. I swatted

him and giggled, as I wiped my face free of the tears that

had started to flow.

"You have made my life worth living. Given me so

much to fight for and look forward to. I've always called

you Mrs. Batiste, but now, it's time that it's recognized

before God and all of our friends and family. You have no

choice but to say yes, so I'll ask this… will you do the

honors of wearing this ring?" he said, flashing me the most

beautiful seven-carat, purple diamond ring housed in a gold band. *My favorite fuckin color!* I thought, while picking the ring up from its place in the gray heart-shaped box and placing it on its new home… my finger. I smiled from ear to ear taking in as much as the ring's beauty as I possibly could with all the water in my eyes. "Baby, is that a yes?" I heard Mo say. I looked back at him forgetting that he had just proposed. I was so fixated on the diamond before me.

"Yes, baby! This ring is fuckin everything!" I exclaimed before jumping in his arms and showering kisses all over his face. "I love you so much, Mo!"

"I love you, too, Mrs. Batiste," he replied back eyeing me. When he licked his lips and bit down on the bottom one, I already knew what time it was. "You done got me hard as motherfucka consenting to be mine forever.

Come here; let's go in the pantry right quick." he said, pointing to the closest door that was right off of the living room. I giggled and then moaned when I thought about that water bottle that he toted between his legs. *I sure could go for some of that.*

Before I could even make one step, Jackie's ugly ass came around the corner clearing her throat like that was supposed to mean something to me. I was about to continue what I was doing before the bitch spoke.

"Everything is a go. Thrilla, I'll have the papers in the morning ready for you to sign along with your new keys." she spoke, never making eye contact with me. How rude?

"Thanks, we'll be there. Now, if you can give us a minute, that would be lovely." I snapped at her Bushwick

Bill looking ass. I grabbed Mo's hand, leading the way to the pantry. I was pissed off with her calling Mo by his boxing name. How unprofessional is that?

"Calm down, Mrs. B," Mo playfully chastised, slapping me on the ass. "Mmm, must be jelly cause jam don't shake like that!" he burst out, causing me to laugh out right at his silly ass.

"Come on; we have a lot to celebrate. This is take one, so know that it's going down tonight!" I bragged, knowing damn well that I was about to give him my all in this closet. Mo's shit was so big that I could only go one round with him if I wanted to be able to walk the next morning. I'd made the same mistake twice of fuckin him all day, and the last time, I wasn't able to walk or sit down without a pillow underneath me.

"Stop fronting; this is me you're talking to. Get your sexy ass on in here and give me what you got." he cracked trying to be funny.

We entered the pantry and closed the door. I lifted my long, flowing maxi skirt up and gave my baby an eyeful of his favorite food. As my baby went down on me, the mad bitch on the other side of the door became a distant memory.

Chapter 6: Chao

"Pots, are you still mad with my daddy?" Breeland asked me for the thousandth time since the fight that Henny and I had outside of the hospital. Since then, it seemed as if I had been in trouble with every female in my life behind it.

Renee was disappointed that I acted in such a way in front of Breeland, which was making me feel worse about the situation. It wasn't my intention to act out in front of my granddaughter, especially with her father being on the receiving end of it. Every time that Bree asked me if I was still upset, it further reminded me of how fucked up it was for me to handle him in front of her.

Chandler, on the other hand, was a different story. I promised her that I wouldn't harm Henny off the strength that he was her baby's father, but I broke that promise. However, I didn't understand why she was upset, because she wasn't even fuckin with him herself, and if I'm being quite honest, as her father, that was one promise that wasn't made to be kept. So, to make the three queens in my life happy with me again, I had decided to invite all the men over so that we could make amends and figure out how we were going to out that bitch ass nigga Zay. I didn't think I could sleep another peaceful night with him being alive.

"No baby girl, I'm not mad at your daddy. In fact, why don't you go help your Nana in the kitchen and prepare the food for your daddy and uncles?" I said, as I placed all of her nail polishes back into her nail bag.

We were in the kid's entertainment room, and I was allowing her to give me a "make-do-over" as she liked to call it. My ladybug always insisted on me playing dress up with her, because she knew that I would bout let her get away with anything. I looked down at the purple and pink polish on my toes and felt in my head at the two pig tales that I had. Shaking my head, I had to chuckle at my spoiled princess.

"So this is what I gotta look forward to when Brai has my little girl?" Chaz said, walking into the room.

"Hey, Uncle Chazzy!" Breeland screamed, as she rushed up to Chaz and hugged him. He picked her up, only to turn her upside down and start tickling her. She was laughing her little head off and was begging for mercy for Chaz to stop his torture. He continued to tickle her and laugh at her squeals until she couldn't hold it anymore and passed gas right in Chaz's face. He dropped Breeland to the ground, and at first, I was ready to go upside his head until I saw that Bree was still laughing and unharmed. Chaz, on the other hand, was kneeled over with his hands on his knees coughing profusely.

"Gah, damn Bree! Your ass smells like a grown ass man!" he said, with his nose bunched up.

"What's up Pots—damn? What's that smell? Smell like that shit y'all be cookin down at the shop," Lil Chaz said, referring to the Chinese Hot Wok that was down in

China Town that our family owned.

"I'm telling my daddy!" Breeland said, still barely

able to contain her laughter.

"Yo, that was you?" Lil Chaz asked Breeland. The

look on his face was one of pure shock. "I thought girls

farts smelled like glitter and cupcakes. Bree's smell like

that homeless man that be down by the station," he joked,

laughing and trying to dap Big Chaz up, but he ended up

getting slapped in the back of his head instead.

"Lil nigga, watch your mouth in front of Lord." Big

Chaz chastised.

"My bad, Pots, I get it from my daddy." he said, as

he flopped down on the oversized black sectional that was

inside of the large room. Renee had really gone all out in

here for the kids. There were in-ground trampolines, gaming systems, all kinds of costumes for dress up, a basketball hoop, and batting cage. The grandkids loved it down here.

"Is everyone here?" I asked Chazman, ready to get this over with so that me and my wife could return back to our regular program. Since the fight with Henny, she'd been making me sleep at the foot of our bed. There was no specific reason and no lesson to be learned from it. I simply had to sleep at the foot, because Nae was petty like that. She wouldn't even let me hold her, so that meant no sex, and I be damned if I slept in another room without her, so the foot was what it was.

"Ya, CJ and Henny were pulling up when we got here." he replied, looking down at his phone. His face had annoyance written all over it. "Lil Chaz, call your mama."

Immediately, I screwed my face up.

Jamiee, Lil Chaz's mother was a handful. She treated

Lil Chaz as collateral to Chazman. She thought that

because she had his son that that automatically made her

his woman. No matter how many times Chaz had cursed

her out, filed restraining orders, and whooped her ass to

put her in her place, she wouldn't budge. She even took it

upon herself to invite herself to family gatherings that we

would have, whether Lil Chaz was there or not. With

Chazman being with Brailynn now, Jamie was playing the

right game with the right one. I'm sure if she got on that

dumb shit around Brai, then Brai wasn't going to have a

problem with setting her crazed ass straight. All I had to

say for Jamie was, tread lightly.

"Who Brai? I thought she was picking me up from here." Lil Chaz said looking disappointed. I loved how close he was to Brailynn. Their relationship was truly one of a kind and it reminded me so much of how Chazman and Renee's relationship was in the beginning.

"Nah, I'm talking about Jamiee. You need to call her so she can stop blowing my phone up." Lil Chaz smacked his lips shaking his head.

"I ain't calling her. You wrong for even making me go over there this weekend. I don't wanna deal with her until I have to." he said looking so serious. Lil Chaz couldn't stand his mother, and he let it be known every time her name was brought up. Knowing that, Chaz still made him visit every weekend, because even though he too couldn't stand Jamiee, he knew what it felt like not to have a mother, and he didn't want that for his son.

"Call your mother boy," I advised him, knowing damn well that he wasn't.

"Come on, Chaz, let's go get this shit started so that it can hurry up and end." I said, as I thought about sleeping at the head of the bed with my wife again. I was going to do everything in my power to ensure that this meeting went as good as the idea sounded.

"Alright, first off, I wanna say that I apologize, Henny, for fighting you in front of Breeland. Not apologizing for laying hands on you, because you knew that was coming, but it shouldn't have went down in front of my granddaughter. Furthermore, we both have other issues that we need to work on together to be rid of, and I'd rather we do that as a team and without being at each other's throats."

I started the meeting off in my man cave with Henny, CJ, Chaz, and I. We were all sitting on the leather sectional with liquor in our glasses and the finest Cuban cigars in the air. Renee had prepared wings, cheese sticks, meatballs, and all kinds of dips and sandwiches. I could have easily had this meeting in my study, but as a piece offering on us becoming a family again, I felt that the men's room would suit us better.

"Cool, all I ask is that y'all two stay neutral while I work to get my girl back. That's it, and that's all." he said, as he threw back what was left of the brown liquor in his glass and poured himself another round of Hennessy, all the while staring both Chazman and I down.

"That right there is a no go; I told you from the jump not to hurt my sister or there were going to be major problems. Luckily for you, I had to promise her not to touch your unappreciative ass. I love you like a brother, but understand that what you and Chand once had is now over. You had the chance to love her and be with her, but you didn't know how. You only get one shot and you missed the free throw." Chazman said, giving Henny the look of death. On the outside looking in, you wouldn't be able to tell that our family has just reunited a short while ago. Chaz and Chand were crazy about each other and stuck to one another like glue.

"I understand that's your sister and you love her, but I ain't letting her go. I love Chandler more than I love getting money. I fouled up, true enough, but I ain't living life without my good thang. Besides, if I can't have your sister, then you ain't bout to be parading around here with mine."

"Nigga, you got me fucked up! Brother or not, I'm killing behind that pussy." Chaz seethed. Henny shot up to his feet, and I knew that if I didn't get a hold onto things that all hell was soon to break loose.

"Aight, y'all chill!" I snapped, growing irritated already by their little spiff. "For the sake of my grandbaby, Henny, you have my blessing once again to make this right and get your family in order. One more fuck-up out of you, and I am going to show you why I am indeed, The Lord of China Town."

Henny slightly nodded, and I could tell that he wanted to say more. I must admit, though, I respected

Henny much more than what I did. He'd been handling himself like any real man would. He fucked up, admitted to his mistakes, and had been working tirelessly to get his lady back. The shit that Chaz and I had been throwing his way hadn't deterred him not once. I salute real niggas, and he had proven himself to be one.

"Moving forward, what's the word on Zay? Our people can't find him anywhere." CJ said, speaking up for the first time since we'd been there. Always quiet and observant. Those two ingredients were the recipe for death.

"Y'all can't find him because we got his ass stashed away begging for his life." I revealed, getting a hard-on from knowing that I had Zay at my mercy. That was the reason why it was hard for me to step down from my position as Lord. I had a taste for blood, and the game quenched it.

"Fair enough, so when we gone handle that?" I watched, as Henny's eyes turned as black as coal. I could only imagine what he was dealing with. I was pissed because of what happened to my daughter, true enough, but I didn't know Zay the way that Henny did. He was double crossed. Now that I was able to set aside our differences, it was clear that the man had the weight of the world on his shoulders.

"Sunday, he is to die on the Sabbath." Chaz replied, wearing an evil grin.

When the chorus of Silks song "Girl You For Me" began to play, we watched as Henny damn near broke his wrist trying to dig into his pocket and retrieve his phone.

"Channy, baby," he said with hope in his eyes. That hope was soon replaced with disappointment. "What do you want, Brai, and where is Chandler?" he said, now with straight attitude.

"Here, and tell her to charge her fuckin phone!" he barked, as he tossed his phone across the room to Chaz and stormed out of the room. I got up to go find him, because although I knew where he was coming from, I needed his head to be clear for what was about to go down in a couple of days.

"Henny!" I yelled out. He was just headed out of the back doors when I caught up to him. I motioned for him to follow me to my study so that we could talk one on one over a drink.

Once there, I poured up his favorite, Henny on ice and Don Julio for me. We sat in silence while I rolled some the finest herbs into one of the grand cigars that I had transported from Cuba. Once I finished and the blunt was lit, I passed it to Henny so that he could have the first puff. He needed it way more than I did.

"I gotta get my woman back. I don't understand how she could just up and leave me like that. She talking about taking Lil Bit from me and everything. She trying to have me out here strung the fuck out, yo. I don't know where the fuck she is. She in her Altima so I can't track her down. I never got around to putting a tracker on her car. She's usually in one of my whips or the truck I got her for graduation. Brailynn ain't saying shit to me about her, Rori is being tight-lipped, and Noni's slow ass just barks at me, indicating that I'm a dog every time I ask her something.

If I lose my girl behind a hoe that don't mean shit to me…" I sat quietly while Henny vented. The shit was straight comedy. I felt where he was coming from solely by putting myself in his shoes. I myself had never been in that position. Renee would never be able to tell you of a time that I had cheated on her. I was many things, but a fool I was not. Besides, had I done that, I wouldn't be here today. She was the only person I feared other than God.

"Look, it hasn't been that long since the incident happened. You gotta give her time. A lot of shit has hit her all at once. She got attacked, the man that she loved cheated on her, and… and," I stuttered over my words, because I was so close to spilling the beans about Chandler being pregnant. Henny looked at me giving me a knowing look.

"So tell me Pops, her ass pregnant? Yo, what the fuck is she playing at!? Why she ain't tell me that shit? Is she thinking about killing my baby!?" he yelled, as he shot to his feet and began walking a hole in my floor. "Chandler is fuckin showing her ass man! I understand her being mad; she has every right to be, but why the fuck is she playing with me about my kids, yo?" I remained silent not saying a word. I hated that this shit was happening. Although I disagreed with hiding the baby from Henny, my loyalty would always and forever be to my daughter.

"Yo, Chao, get her ass on the phone. We need to talk about this shit. I'm telling you right now, you might as well get those choppas ready, cause if she says some shit that I don't like, I'm breaking her fuckin neck!" he seethed.

Empty. That's what I thought about his threats. I tried to

hold in my laughter, but I couldn't resist the joke.

"Now, now, let's calm down. You're assuming right

now. I never confirmed or denied that she is indeed

pregnant. You jumped to conclusions on that. You two

need to sit down and have a serious talk." Henny sighed

and took a seat on the plush red leather. "Listen son, in due

time, it will all work out. Give her time to accept what has

happened. You all have Breeland, so you have to talk at

some point. You messed up, and if this is something that

you want, then you should stop at nothing to get it back." I

advised him with a pat on the back.

I left out of the study in search for my wife.

Listening to Henny's problems had me wanting to show

her of one of the reasons why she should forever stay…

maybe two if I eat it right and she allows me to slide in

between those golden brown thighs.

Chapter 7. Hendrix.

The worst thing that a nigga could do during a breakup is to drink liquor, blow Dro, and listen to throwback 90's R&B. I had been riding around getting fucked up ever since I left the luncheon at Mama Nae and Chao's house.

Everyone was telling me to wait and be patient, but when your heart was broken, all you wanted was relief, and right now, my relief didn't want to have nothing to do with me. So this fifth of Henny and a blunt filled with the finest green was accompanying me, being my rider, riding

shotgun in the shark-colored Porsche I was pushing for

the day. With only one person in mind, I went to the one

place that I knew she would be.

I sat outside of the building of Chandler's job and

thought about what I was about to do. My emotions were

running wild, and my heart was feeling more heavy than it

had been since finding out that all my shit had been aired.

I picked up the bottle of Henny and put it to my lips. I

tossed my head back and took a gulp of the warm brown

liquor, then thought for a second. *I can either sit here and give*

this girl the time she needs to get over me or I can boss the fuck up

and show her ass that I'm sorry. I pondered over what I

should do, but the decision really wasn't that hard.

I lit up my blunt to give myself a second to calm my nerves a bit. I had to prepare myself in case she really didn't want to fuck with me anymore. I relaxed in my seat and turned up the radio. I continued to smoke and pray that what I was about to do wouldn't get her fired, because Chand loved this pissy ass job, and if I was the cause to get her terminated, then she really wouldn't take my ass back.

Emotions make you cry sometimes

Emotions make you sad sometimes

Emotions make you glad sometimes

But most of all they make you fall in love

I nodded my head to that H-town, feeling the fuck out of the song. It was always that good old school and

R&B that made a man sit down and really think about the shit that was going on with him and his lady. Right now, I was on the same shit that these niggas were on. If I had to, I would sing to my girl just like them, on bended knee, in the rain, in front of her friends, with green eggs and ham, hell anywhere as long as she could see that I was a fuck-up that was truly sorry for hurting her. That was when it hit me.

I had been trying to talk to Chand since the shit hit the fan, and she had been avoiding me. I needed her not only to listen, but to make her feel the emotions that I was feeling, and what better way than to do that than through a song? Chand was a phenomenal singer, and I knew that, without a doubt, she would feel and appreciate this shit.

Without much more thought, I put my blunt out and turned my car off. I popped in a piece of gum and sprayed some cologne on, not wanting to give none of these old ass folks a contact high, although it might actually make them feel better. I got out of the car, stumbling a bit from drinking and being seated for so long. I fixed my clothes then headed inside. It was a beautiful day outside, and I dressed the part in a part in a pair of Nike gray sweat shorts, white Nike tank, and a pair of all white Nike Huaraches. My gold chain, watch, and diamond earrings were all the jewelry that I had on. Feeling like new money, because I was about to be in the presence of my queen, I added a smile to my face.

I pulled the door open and was immediately greeted by a group of old women attempting to do the cupid shuffle. Most were moving like zombies, but some I could tell that they used to get down back in their day. I stood watching them for a minute, then I went to the front desk station to check in.

This wasn't my first time being here. I used to come here and kick it with Chand on her lunch break. I even had the pleasure of getting to know a few of the elders that resided here. Mrs. Ann was my favorite, so I signed in as a visitor to see her. No matter how much I hated this job for Chand, she loved it, and I didn't want to run the risk of getting her wrote up. The nurse gave me my pass, and I went down the hall and to the elevators, then pressed the number two for the second floor. I exited when the doors opened and made a left all the way down to the last door on the hall. I knocked twice before entering and caught one of my favorite girls sitting in her favorite rocking chair watching her westerns.

"Hey, Mrs. Ann. How you doing?" I asked, coming into view and taking a seat on the sofa chair that she had placed in her room. Mrs. Ann looked over to me and smiled genuinely.

"You wouldn't have to ask how I was doing if you stopped by more often. Feel like I haven't seen you in a month of Sundays." she fussed, getting up out of her seat and pulling me up to give her a hug. The embrace was warm and made me sober up just a tad.

"That's why I'm here to see my old lady." I followed Mrs. Ann to the kitchen area of her room. She was one of the few on the premises that had extended additions on their rooms. For what it was worth, Mrs.

Ann was a great cook, and I could smell the food she had

on the stove in the air. I was right on time as my stomach

grumbled. I was coming down with the munchies that the

Dro that I smoked earlier left behind.

"Now why you tell that tale? I know what's going

on with you and Miss Pretty." she said calling me out on

my bullshit. I laughed at the nickname that she had given

Chandler. I thought that it was cute and that it fit my baby

perfectly.

"I'm serious. I had to stop and see how you been

doing." I took a seat at the table and waited for her reply.

Mrs. Ann might have been old, but she was far from a

dummy.

"Uh huh, I know better boy. She'll be here at the

end of her shift. You got an hour to spare? Are you

hungry?" she asked, but I knew that she was gon' fix me a plate anyways despite my answer. Still, I answered with manners and watched her move around the kitchen.

"Here. Now, tell me why'd you do it, and what's the plan to get her back." she said, after sitting a big ass bowl of chicken and dumplings in front of me. On the side was a saucer of cornbread, and next to it was a tall glass of sweet tea. I quickly said grace, something I picked up from Chand, and immediately began to dig in. Mrs. Ann sat across from me and patiently waited for me to answer.

"I did it for one of the most dumbest reasons ever, Mrs. Ann." I said, looking at her but still putting a dent into my food.

"Well… what was it?" she pushed, with her hand falling on her thick hip. If this was anyone else, I would have shut this conversation down for them being so fucking nosey, but I knew Mrs. Ann was anything but. She would give you what you needed to hear. The real. She wasn't the type to sugar coat shit, and that's what I needed. I pushed my near empty bowl back and wiped my hand on the towel that was on the table for that specific use. Rubbing my hands down my face, I became transparent, ready to soak up the wisdom of someone far older than the ones available in my circle.

"I didn't feel like she needed me, and before you start, I know that I'm a man, but for your woman to walk around as if she wears the pants for someone like me is a lot. I'm so used to taking care of everyone around me, and for me to have someone like Chandler that I love more than anything next to kin not need me for anything is hard. It's a blow to my ego if I'm being honest. She unmans me, makes me feel as if I'm not doing enough for her. I used to buy her shit and would have to fight her to take it. I have to go behind her back to pay all of her bills because if I give her the money for it, it'll be lying on the dresser when I get back home. How am I supposed to be a man and take care of her when she doesn't let me?" I sighed heavily and went back to the bowl of dumplings that Mrs. Ann had just refilled. It felt good getting my true feelings off of my chest. Only real providers with real independent women would know what I was going through.

"First off, I don't think that there is anything wrong with you feeling the way that you feel. The problem is that you lacked to communicate that with your woman. If you're so much of a man, Hendrix, then what stopped you from pulling her aside and stressing these things to her? And if you say your pride, then let me tell you baby, you are in the wrong business. There is no pride in love. When you're in love, your ego shouldn't exist. You talk things out with your partner and together the two of you come to a conclusion. You young folks kill me bringing all of these factors that don't matter into your relationship. Ya pride and ya ego, ha! If you're going to love someone, you do it without consequence."

I sat back in my chair and rubbed my hands down my face. Mrs. Ann just said a mouthful. I was feeling more fucked up, because I was the man in this and should have been set my shit aside and looked at what I was doing wrong before I cheated. Now that the damage had been done, I was going to do whatever it took to get my girl back, and this time, I was playing for keeps.

KNOCK, KNOCK!

"Hey Mrs. Ann, it's 'bout that time for me to go. I was just coming to--,"

At the sound of my baby's voice, I stood up from the chair that I was sitting in and took in her thick frame. Chand was looking good as fuck in her purple and gray scrubs. The top fit loosely, but the pants were hugging her ass like they were in a ten-year relationship. Her usual bare face had light makeup on it, I'm assuming to cover the barely there bruises from her attack. Thinking about that shit sent my heart rate to speed up a bit more than what it

already was. She looked at me from head to toe with her

mouth wide open. Behind her eyes were a mixture of lust

and hate, and that bothered me. "What are you doing

here, Hendrix?" she asked, well more like snarled.

"I… I was just umm…" I couldn't even get my

thoughts right to even talk. The plan that I came in here

with had been completely forgotten.

"Well… go on." I could hear Mrs. Ann

encouraging me, but shit, I honestly couldn't think of

anything to say. I opened my mouth and just let the first

thing that came flow out.

"Girl, you know I- I- I- love you. No matter what

you do. And I hope you understand me, every word I say

is true. Cause I love you… baby I'm thinking of you tryin

to be more of a man for you." I opened my eyes that I didn't even know where closed to Chand and Mrs. Ann laughing their asses off. I knew I was drunk and off-key, but still, they didn't have to laugh in my face like that.

"I'm sorry, son; I thought you had a speech. I don't mean to laugh, but that was unexpected. I'm going to the bathroom; you two you need to talk." Mrs. Ann said before she left out of the kitchen giving Chand and I some space. I looked over at her, and she was back to looking grimacing.

"Henny, even though I know that we should, right now for me is not a good time to talk. I have all these emotions and other shit that I have to sort through before we can do that. Right now, I really just want to focus on Bree and our co-parenting schedule." she said. Her mentioning co-parenting pissed me the hell off, for the simple fact that she meant that shit.

"Speaking of, how the hell you gone take Lil Bit and leave like that?"

"Just like I said I was. Text me a location, and I'll meet you there with her tomorrow." she said, putting her jacket on and collecting her work bag from behind Mrs. Ann's couch. She said nothing else before she left out. Not even goodbye to Mrs. Ann, who was just now coming out of the bathroom.

"Is she gone? How was the talk?" she asked. I could tell by the sympathetic look on her face that she already knew the answer. "Everything is going to be fine. She's still hurting. In the meantime, work on you. You're the foundation; you have to be solid or else the two of you will continue to crack and crumble." I nodded my head in agreement and embraced her in a hug. Mrs. Ann was really helpful to me today, and I truly appreciated the jewels she dropped on me.

"I'ma get out of here. I'll stop by to see you soon; I promise." I said. I kissed her cheek then headed for the door.

"Bring that beautiful little girl with you next time." she called out.

"Yes ma'am." I replied, and with that, I headed out of the building to pick back up where I had left off. This Henny and loud ain't never let me down.

Chapter 8. Chandler

I was laid out on the chaise chair that rested in the corner of my bedroom. Meshell Ndegeocelle "Bitter" album was on repeat and played softly in the background as I sat and stared out of the window. Breeland and I had been at my old apartment for the past four days, and she was adjusting better than what I expected her to. I didn't know if taking her from her father was the best idea, but I wasn't trying to leave her behind. I truly looked at that little girl like she was mine. I couldn't see myself not being in her life so taking her with me was the only option that was left.

Listening to the rain beat outside, I allowed my mind to drift off to happier times as Meshell sang about no one being faithful. My shaky fingers played with my bottom lip to keep me from crying. Lord knows that I was tired of baring my soul, but dammit, I just couldn't help it. The tears fell, but a smile came soon after when I thought about the time that Hendrix, Bree, and I went to the park to feed the ducks. We were having a good time until we ran out of bread and the ducks began to chase after us. I never heard a man scream so loud until that day. The tears continued to fall as more memories came, and as if God himself was saying "snap out of it", a loud clap of thunder sounded off

nearly causing me to jump out of my skin.

"Mommy, I'm scared; it's thundering too hard."

Breeland's soft voice rang out jarring me from my

thoughts. I looked up to see her coming into my bedroom

with her Disney Princess blanket in tow. I hurried to wipe

my face free from the tears that were coming down in

boatloads. I hated for Bree to see me cry.

"Come on little scary," I cracked, and she giggled. I

picked her up, and together, we got into my bed. I snuggled

with my baby girl, and soon, she was fast asleep.

"I remember, when you filled my heart with joy,

was I blind to the truth just there to fill the space,

cause now you have no interest in anything I have to say

and I have allowed you to make me feel dumb…"

I listened to the lyrics that were playing in the background, and a sense of sadness washed over me. The life that I pictured with the love of my life was shot. I didn't have a backup plan; the plan was to love Henny for the rest of my life. He had to go and fuck that all up.

"What kind of fool am I that you so easily set me aside, you made a fool of me, tell me why…" his touch, I missed that.

As I stared back out of the window and watched the rain knock hard against the glass, Hendrix would be holding me right now, spooning me from the back with his arms wrapped tight around me as if he let me go, then I'll slip right through his fingers. How ironic is that?

"You made a fool of me, tell me why…" the words to the

song began to play in my head like a mantra that I so badly

wanted to forget. *"You made a fool of me…"*

I couldn't take it anymore as I shot up from the bed,

face wet from the ocean of tears that were pouring down

my face. I went into my bathroom and stared at my

reflection in the mirror. My stitches were beginning to

dissolve, and I only had minor bruising now. Despite all of

that, even I could still see the beauty that lied beneath so

why wasn't I enough? Why couldn't I be loved? I scanned

every part of my body looking for the reason, becoming

more insecure by the second.

All of a sudden I had the urge to do something

drastic, something that I had never done before. I was filled

to the brim with emotions, and by picking up the scissors, I felt a sense of empowerment. I pulled the hair tie from my hair and let my hair hang over my shoulders and down my back.

"You say that you don't care but we made love, tell me why,"

Images of my love standing behind me, whispering in my ear how much he loved me, staring down into my eyes and capturing my soul replayed in my head as the song continued to play.

"You made a fool of me…"

I closed my eyes tightly and shook my head from left to right trying to rid myself of the memories. I thought back to the video, and my mind raced as it played images of my love giving someone else what was supposed to only be for me.

"Aahhh!" I screamed out, as I lifted my hand that held the scissors and snipped at my hair viciously.

"You made a fool of me, tell me why"

I continued to cut. My hands were starting to hurt from holding the scissors so tight, but I didn't let that stop me. I went mad and took my anger out on my hair. I was tired of love hurting me.

"Tell me why."

"Chand! What are you doing, Mama!" I heard someone call out as I continued to cry and snip. The sound that the scissors made when they cut my hair was giving me a high that I couldn't quite explain. "Chand, have you lost your fuckin mind!?" I still didn't answer. I couldn't answer. Had I really lost my mind?

"Give me this shit!" I turned to the entrance and saw all of my girls looking back at me. Of course, it was Rorilynn who took the scissors out of my hand. We all just stood there for a minute holding each other's gazes until I finally broke down. Brailynn was the first to run to my side as I collapsed in her arms and balled like a baby.

"Noni, run her some bath water." Rori called out as she joined me at my side. She and Brailynn helped me to undress and climb into the hot water that was filled with jasmine bath seeds.

We all sat in silence or at least that's how it seemed. I was so out of it that I couldn't focus on the conversation if they were having one. My heart was shattered. This was a pain that I wanted to steer clear from; even the rejection from my first love in high school didn't hurt this bad. I sat as if I was a statue all numb-like as Brailynn washed me up. When I got out of the tub, she helped me to dress in a pair of gray Nike fitted sweats and a white Nike sports bra with the matching jacket. Rori took me down to the kitchen where she cut my hair evenly and then washed it.

I cried silently the whole time as I thought about what led me to cut over eleven inches of my hair. *Why the fuck did I have to fall in love?* I thought to myself. When we were through, I let Noni blow dry and style my hair since she knew what she was doing when it came to shorter lengths. I no longer had long hair flowing down my back. I was now rocking a very short cut that put you in the mind of Miranda Brooke's wedding photos. The finger waves that Noni did had me looking extra feminine and sexy. I actually liked it; I would even love it if I wasn't so against the "*L*" word.

"Ma, on some real shit. You take this day and cry your pretty little heart out, but make sure that this is your last time crying over this shit. I don't want no more tears over Henny's ass. You have too much to look ahead to. You have a beautiful daughter, who looks up to you, and she doesn't want to see you cry all the time. You have a baby growing inside of you that feeds off of your energy. If you cry the whole time that you're pregnant, don't you know that your baby will come out being a crybaby as well? We don't want that. You don't want that. Ain't nobody trying to baby sit a crybaby." Rori said, as I giggled a little. I nodded my head and wiped the tears from my face. She was right, and I was so grateful to have friends that loved and cared for me the way that they did.

Around noon, the girls and I decided to turn the day into a girl's day with the four of us and my baby girl. We had set up a spa in my living room with pedicure tubs and gel polish dryers for our nails. We had Rotel and chips, sub sandwiches, meatballs and party wings. Brai and Rori drunk margaritas, while Noni and I turned up on green tea and Lil bit was in heaven drinking all the chocolate milk that she wanted.

"Brai, what's the matter? You're over there turbo texting." Rori called out, drawing all of our attention to Brailynn.

"It's Chaz's ass. I'm so sick of arguing with him about having a baby." she huffed. The news was welcomed.

Not because my girl and brother were having problems, never that. But because I was finally able to give my mind a break from thinking about Henny.

"Do you not want to give him a baby?" I asked, hoping that she spoke the right answer.

"Of course I want his baby! It's just that I'm so fuckin scared, Chand. What type of mother can I be when I really didn't have one there to teach me? I had to look to your mom and my brother for anything girl related. On top of that fear, what if after I have this man's baby, he ups and leaves me? I don't feel comfortable having his child without a bigger commitment in place first." she stressed.

"So in other words, you want him to propose marriage, and or get married before having a baby?" Rori pried.

"Exactly. Coming from what I been through, I need that type of commitment. Chaz is saying that I don't love him, because I won't have his baby, and it's starting to make me feel horrible. I mean, what am I to say? I'm not giving you a baby until you marry me? It's like blackmail. I want Chaz to propose when he's ready and for the simple fact that he knows that I'm so fucking amazing that he is not going to find a love like mine anywhere else."

"I agree, but you do need to let him know your outlook. Your ultimate goal is marriage. Have a talk with him and see if that at least is in his future plans."

"I agree with Rori, but knowing how crazy my brother is about you, I wouldn't even stress too much about that. Trust me, he is planning on trappin your ass anyway that he can." I laughed, but was very serious about the matter. Chazman was straight gone off of Brai. I knew

that for him, putting a baby up in her was ensuring him

that he would have her forever.

"I don't know why, but I believe you, Chand." she

replied. We continued to talk and gossip about nothing in

particular until my meet-up with Henny crossed my mind.

"I'm supposed to drop Breeland off to Hendrix--,"

"Roof roof!" I was cut off by barking noises coming

from ZaNoni.

"Noni, the fuck is wrong with you?" I asked, looking

at her crazy ass like she was just that... crazy.

"Ain't nothing wrong with me. Finish what you were

saying, Ma," she said, as she continued to stuff her face.

Her little belly was getting out there, and I couldn't stop myself from leaning over and rubbing it.

"Like I was saying, at six this evening, I have to drop Bree off to Henny--."

"Roof!"

"Noni! Why the hell are you barking!?" I exclaimed. I promise you my friend had no sense.

"I thought we were talking dog. Every time you say his name, I can't help but to bark." she said with a shrug of her shoulders. That was why I loved her ass!

"So you're saying that Henny—," Brai started.

"Roof roof!"

"Is a dog?" she finished, barely able to contain her laughter. Noni just shrugged.

"Henny." Rori said testing her.

"Roof," Noni replied.

"Hendrix," I said egging her on.

"Roof roof!" Noni clapped back. That was it; I couldn't hold it in anymore as we all cracked up laughing. I didn't even bother to finish what I had to say.

The day went by fast as we enjoyed each other's company. This was exactly what I needed to lift my spirits up. I was looking good and feeling even better as I put on my shoes to go drop Lil Bit off. She was lollygagging around like she didn't want to go, and I had to tell her to get dressed twice. Now, she was acting as if she couldn't find her shoes when the shoe box was right on top of her bed.

"Bree, are you ready babe?" I asked, as I tied the strings to my white Nike Roshe Runners. I kept on what I had on from earlier and just threw on silver accessories which included my Fossil watch, diamond-studded earrings, and a solitaire diamond necklace. I walked into Breeland's room, and she wore the biggest pout on her face that could bring any mother to her knees.

"What's the matter, Lil Bit? Aren't you ready to see Daddy?" I asked, as I kneeled down to put her shoes on. She was dressed similarly to me in a purple Nike jogging suit, with a gray Nike running shirt underneath. On her feet, were a pair of silver and white Air Max 90's that I assumed were her favorite shoes because she wanted to wear them with everything.

"Of course, I wanna see Daddy, but I'm going to miss you. I don't really wanna go." she sniffled and rubbed her nose that had turned red just that fast.

"Baby girl, you will be back before you know it. I know you'll miss me, but right now, Daddy misses you. You have to go and keep him company okay?" she nodded her head letting me know that she understood. I stood to my feet and pulled her into my arms. I felt like crying because I really didn't want my baby girl to leave. I enjoyed our days together, and as soon as she was out of my sight, I was going to be counting down to the day that she came back.

"Come on; I think your daddy is waiting." I said, as I led the way out of her room.

I was meeting Henny at Mr. Murph's, a local pizza buffet that we often frequented with Lil Bit. The closer we got, the sweatier my palms became. When we pulled into the lot, I spotted Henny's Porche Panarama and parked two cars over, because I wasn't quite ready to see him just yet. I pulled the visor down so that I could look into the mirror; I had to get a good look at my reflection and remind myself who the fuck I was. Now wasn't the time to cry and be weak.

"Let's shake and bake, Lil Mama." I called out to Breeland, as I got out of my two-door Altima and lifted the seat up to let her out of the back. When I left Henny, I really left him. The day that I checked out of the hospital, I had Rori take me by the house that Hendrix and I once shared, I got my car that I had before we got together, scooped Bree from my parents' house, and together, we went back to my old apartment. That was our home now.

"Hey baby girl!" I damn near jumped out of my skin when I heard Hendrix speak to Breeland. I didn't know that he was standing behind us this whole time. I watched the two of them engage in a hug, and it warmed my heart to see the love that he had for her. I subconsciously rubbed my belly and thought about the love that I was developing for the baby that was growing inside of me. I wasn't planning on telling Hendrix just yet; I had my first doctor's appointment tomorrow morning, and I planned to let him know Monday evening when we met again to swap off Bree.

"Walk us to the car, Mommy?" he asked, looking at me with those big, beautiful, hazel eyes that I loved to get lost in. I held his gaze until his eyes dropped down to roam my body.

"Yo, Ma, you cut your hair?" he asked like it was the shock of the world. I just stared at him not wanting to say anything for fear that the dam in my eyes would break and my real emotions would come out. "It looks good, baby. Damn good." he said, as he reached for my hair. Before he could touch it, I slapped his hand away and turned up the attitude.

"Are we walking to your car or not?" I asked, as I looked down at my watch, giving him the impression that I had better stuff to do with my time. Henny gave me a look that I never wanted see upon his face again. Hurt definitely didn't fit him. He tucked his bottom lip, then looked down at Breeland, who was looking up at us waiting. He nodded and walked off to his car as I followed. I was ready to hug

and kiss my baby bye so that I could go home and throw

part two of my pity party.

"Come here, Mommy's Princess," I cooed, once we

made it to Henny's car. I picked Breeland up, and the both

of us hugged like we were never going to see each other

again. "Remember what I said, okay? These days are going

to fly by. I'll see you Monday after school." I assured her. I

puckered my lips and she kissed them before climbing

down looking like she was about to cry. *Fuckin Henny!* I

helped her into her seat and placed her seat belt on. Once

she was secure, I closed the door and turned ready to walk

in the direction of my car.

"Baby, wait!" Henny called out, as he grabbed my

hand before I could make one step.

"Give me my hand back, and call me by my name please." I snapped.

"Look yo, how long are you going to keep this up? You done left me, took my kid, placed us on this bullshit ass schedule... Think about what this shit is doing to your daughter, Chand! Every time we do this, that same sad look is going to be on her face, and it's all because of you! Baby, I know I fucked up; I fucked up bad, but please Ma, y'all gotta come home. This is the worst thing that you could have ever done. How you gone leave me like that? Leave me broken like this. A nigga ain't eating, ain't breathing right cause he ain't got you in his life. I'm so sorry for hurting you; I promise that shit will never happen again. Just please come home, Ma," I fought hard. So hard to keep my tears at bay. I wanted to believe him, but how could I? I didn't know what was fact or fiction. There was

no way that I could be in a relationship like that.

"I'm pregnant." I blurted out, not really knowing

why. I didn't know what else to say and the baby had

crossed my mind.

"Word, damn Ma. Look at God!" he said, smiling

from ear to ear. His perfect smile and white teeth were

damn near blinding me. "Come on, baby, get in the car. I

promise I am going to make all of this up to you. I know I

have a long ways to go to earn your trust, but I'm not

giving up on us, on our family. I'm so happy--,"

"Hendrix, no. I'm not going with you, and we aren't

getting back together. I told you about the baby, because

you have a right to know. When he or she gets here, it will

be the same thing that's going on now; only difference is

that we will have two kids." I said, hating that I had to rain

on his parade, but he needed to know that my intentions

weren't for us to get back together.

"Man, Chand… you got me fucked up! So you really

going to do this to me? You gone take the baby away from

me too!? That's foul yo! I know I fucked up but do I really

deserve this? You denying me of my kids ain't wassup, Ma,

straight up!"

"The baby is not even here yet, Henny! You're

raving and ranting for nothing!"

"How the fuck can you fix your mouth to say that?

The woman I love is pregnant with my baby, and you're

saying that you don't want me there to watch your belly get

big, I can't be at doctors' visits to hear his heartbeat? I

missed out on all of that with Breeland, Ma, and you're

wanting to snatch that from me again?" he asked, as I

watched the tears form in his eyes. I couldn't hold back

anymore. The moment I blinked, my face became soaked

in a sea of salt water.

"I'm... I'm sorry." I choked out. We stood staring

until he could no longer take it anymore. I watched as he

tucked his lips and looked off nodding his head. When I

saw a tear fall down his left cheek, I turned and hauled ass

back to my car. I knew that if I was to stick around for a

minute longer then I would cave and end up wrapping my

arms around, comforting, and loving him.

The drive back to my house was rather quick due to

the fact that I couldn't focus and ended up running several

red lights and stop signs. As soon as I entered my home, I

went to my radio that was placed at the bottom of the

entertainment center underneath the 70" plasma screen television. I pressed play and let my break-up mix speak the pains of my heart for me. Mariah Carey's "H.A.T.E.U." began to play and it was the perfect song. I flopped down and listened to the lyrics.

Who knew that love could hurt so bad? Was my last thought before I drifted off into a not so good sleep.

I awoke the next morning feeling like I had a love sick hangover. The same way that I felt when I went to bed last night was the same way that I felt this morning. I turned over onto my back, off of my side to get more comfortable. That's when I noticed that I didn't even make it to my bedroom the night before. I was still on the couch and the radio was still softly playing.

Glancing at the clock, I noticed that I was running late for my doctor's appointment to confirm my pregnancy and find out the exact date as to how far along I was. When I was admitted to the hospital after my attack, the doctors discovered my pregnancy and gave me an estimate of how far I was due, to what their machines would allow. I now had to follow up with my own OBGYN to get all the details behind it.

While I got dressed, I was wishing that Hendrix and I were on good terms. I wanted him to be here with me, but my pride would never allow me to voice this to him. Once my feelings got hurt, it was like I had no control over what took place in my mind. My heart could be telling me one thing, but my mind took reign over it. I eat, think, and breathe with a broken heart. Therefore, a lot of stuff that I did came out as me being spiteful and heartless, but that

wasn't the case at all. I simply just didn't know how to deal

with all of this. Pushing those thoughts aside, I arose from

the couch and went to my bedroom to get dressed.

I moved around, sluggishly brushing my teeth and

washing my face. I took a hot shower, and once I was out,

I took time lotioning my body down in a coconut oil and

shea butter mixture. I then went into my closet and threw

on some underwear and a bra, both from Victoria's

Secret. Having little time to finish getting ready, I grabbed

the first pair of jeans I saw, which were a pair of charcoal

gray spandex pants that zipped at the ankle, a fitted white

shirt, and black blazer. Keeping the studs in my ear from

last night, I wrapped my Michael Kors bangles around my

wrist and put on my Steve Madden pointed toe black

suede heels. Walking over to the vanity that sat catty

corner in my bedroom, I sat down and moisturized my

face. I opted out of makeup and lathered my lips with my

EOS lip balm.

Finally, taking my rat tail comb off the vanity, I fixed

my wet and wavy hair. It was somewhat still intact from the

waves Noni had put into it yesterday, and my shower this

morning made my hair super wavy so luckily it wasn't hard

to manage. I grabbed my phone, keys, and purse and

headed out of the door on my way to my first prenatal visit.

When I got there, I immediately checked in seeing as

though I was late and had to take fifteen minutes to fill out

paperwork. It took longer than usual to get called to the

back. I sat in the waiting room and watched the many

families come and go. Even though, I wasn't the only single

mother there, I felt a sense of sadness that I was going through this by myself. I always thought that this was something that Hendrix and I would always do together. I thought about what he said yesterday, and his words still cut through me like a knife. Was I really that bitter that I was going to take away from him something that he wanted so badly? I didn't want to be that girl. I wanted for Henny to know how it felt to be hurt, but I didn't want to be the one doing the hurting. I still very much loved him; I just wanted to take the lesson learned from our relationship and move on.

"Chandler Mengyao," A blonde headed, short, white nurse called out my name, as I stood and made my way towards her. "Good morning, follow me right this way."

she spoke kindly. I followed her down the hall until we stopped in front of the scale.

"Okay, I am going to get you to take your shoes off, and I'll hold your belongings while I take down your weight." she said, with her hands, out ready to hold my purse and heels.

"That's okay, Miss. I'll hold it for her." My body went hot then numb when I turned around and saw Henny standing there looking like the best thing my eyes had ever laid upon. I wanted to be mad and throw him an attitude, but his Versace cologne invading my nostrils had me wanting to turn over a new leaf, literally. I was prepared to turn around, bend over, and allow him to take me right here and now.

"Okay, Ms. Mengyao, watch your step." The nurse smiled at the both of us. I stepped on the scale and closed my eyes not wanting to see the pounds that I know I had gained.

Once my weight was taken, I placed my shoes back onto my feet, snatched my purse out of Hendrix's hand, and followed the nurse, who I now knew was named Lisa, to the room that the examination would take place in. All while ignoring Henny.

"Okay, sweetie. I am going to need you to undress from the waist down and place this blanket across your lap to cover up with." Ms. Lisa said, before walking out of the room and leaving Henny and I alone.

I followed directions, taking off everything from the waist down and draping my clothes across the vacant chair that was next to the one that Henny was in. The tension in the room was growing thicker and thicker until I just couldn't take it anymore.

"What the fuck are you doing here, Hendrix?" I gritted, pissed that he hadn't even tried to explain himself.

"First of all, don't curse at me. I told you yesterday that you had me fucked up, I'mma be in my baby's life, Chand, whether you like it or not, so get used to seeing me at every appointment."

"How did you even know where to come? I never told you the location, building, or time." I asked, finding it weird that he knew exactly where I was.

"Don't worry about it. Just know that you're fucked now. Ain't no getting rid of me. You might as well go ahead, find your white dress, and get ready to say yes." he quipped. Before I could tell him off, there was a knock on the door, followed by Mr. John and Nurse Lisa entering the room.

"Good morning, how are you? I'm Dr. John Ford." He greeted Hendrix with his hand outstretched for him to take. Henny took it with hesitance and introduced himself as the father of my child.

"Okay, Chandler. I've been seeing you since you were sixteen, and now, you're having a baby. I guess I really am getting old," he chuckled, as his big belly shook along with his long, nicely trimmed, gray beard. I had watched Mr. John age over the years, and he still looked just as sexy now as he did when I was sixteen. He was a tall, Caucasian man, who once had a nice, toned body, but he now had a belly on him. It did nothing to take away the charm that was etched on his face. His deep blue eyes and salt and pepper hair were tapered and shaped as if he had stopped by his barber on his way into work this morning. He had a pretty, white smile with straight teeth, and given his age, it was a wonder that they were all his.

"The fuck are you looking at? Fix your face, yo!" my ogling was interrupted by Hendrix raising his voice at me. Fuck! I was caught red-handed. Apparently, while I was looking at Mr. John, Henny was looking at me. Rolling my eyes at him, I focused my attention on the nurse and the doctor in the room.

"I need you to lay back so that we can see what's cooking down here." Mr. John said with a chuckle, and I could tell that it was an attempt to lighten the tension that was apparent between Hendrix and me.

"Wait a minute; let her do it." Henny said pointing to Nurse Lisa.

"I don't mean any harm, but I don't know her like that, and Mr. John has been seeing me since I was sixteen years old. I'm comfortable with him," I said not hiding the attitude.

"Listen yo, this shit ain't about to fly. If ole girl ain't gone do it, then John is about to show me how. You ain't bout to cheat on me in my face." he fumed, while standing to his feet and grabbing a rubber glove from the box that sat on the counter in the room.

"Seriously, no! Mr. John, I am so sorry, but can Nurse Lisa please continue with doing my check-up, please?" I asked, hating to be put in this situation. I was so embarrassed that I couldn't even look at Mr. John while I asked the question.

"Sure, little one. I get these types all the time." Both he and Lisa chuckled.

"Hmph." Henny let out, and I wanted to slap the shit out of him. Bastard always ended up getting his way.

I laid back and let nurse Lisa do her thing. Hendrix and I both asked any and everything that came to mind. Me, so much so that I could get used to her prying in my pussy. Henny, just because he was genuinely concerned. *Go fuckin figure.*

"Okay, Chandler, I was informed that while you were in the hospital they gave you an estimate of how far along you are and they told you around eight weeks or so. Doing a thorough check, we've concluded that you are in fact ten weeks pregnant. We are going to get the transducer in here so that we can see your little bug on the big screen." Nurse Lisa beamed as did I. Despite everything that was going on, I was happy to be becoming a mother for the second time. Mr. John and Lisa both left out of the room, and Hendrix and I were left alone once again.

"When we leave here, we need to go talk." he said. I ignored him but knew that he was right.

Several awkward minutes later, Lisa came in with an ultrasound machine following her. I laid back on the bed and watched as she squirted cool blue gel over the lower part of my stomach. I tensed at the cold sensation.

"I'm sorry; I forgot to warn you that it may be a little cold," Nurse Lisa said sincerely. "Okay, Mommy and Daddy... if you look right here... that is your baby." she informed, pointing to the screen. When I looked and saw my baby, I couldn't stop my eyes from crying.

"How did I not know this?" I asked. From the look on the screen, I could see a clear image of my baby's head and fingers in black and white.

"It happens sometimes. You're not showing, but your stomach is as hard as a rock. A lot of times, you can carry your baby in different areas. If your hips have spread recently, then that's because of the baby. Just watch; you are going to blow up overnight." Mr. John explained.

"Channy, you got a grown ass man in your stomach. That nigga head big as hell; he got that shit from your Chinese side." Henny said, as he looked at the screen with fascination. Mr. John and Nurse Lisa thought it was funny and couldn't help but to laugh at his crazy ass.

"Would you guys like some pictures?" Nurse Lisa asked; I nodded my head and let her do her before I wiped the gel off, and she and Mr. John left out of the room.

I got up and went to get dressed, but Hendrix pulled me into his chest from behind.

"I need you, Chandler." he mumbled into my neck, kissing the sensitive spot behind my ear. My knees betrayed me by becoming weak. I caved into his chest and allowed his mouth to reclaim territory that wasn't his.

"Henny, let's go so that we can talk," I said.

"Mmm," he moaned like it was pure torture to turn my neck loose. Once he let me go, I scrambled to get dressed slipping into my clothes in record breaking time. I grabbed my purse and keys and flew out the room and doctors office wanting to put as much distance between Henny and I as possible.

"Damn, girl. Slow your ass down. Meet me at the auto shop; we can talk there since it's close to Bree's school, and I have to pick her up in a couple of hours." I simply nodded and got into my car. I cranked the car and turned the air on high even though it was chilly outside. My body was hot all over starting from my center, leading up to my breasts that were aching to be kissed and stopping at my neck where Hendrix's wet kisses still lingered on my skin. *Get it together, Chand. Get your shit together.*

Thirty minutes later, I pulled into the lot of Hendrix and CJ's auto body repair shop. It was one of the many legit buildings that they had as a way to keep the police off their asses. Walking into the shop, I bypassed the garage where about five men were working and the guest that were waiting on their vehicle. I went into the side door that led to the hall where CJ and Henny's offices were.

When I got to Hendrix's door, I knocked twice then walked in. He wasn't in there, so I took my seat in front of his desk and waited patiently for him to enter. I looked around the room and noticed how much I played a role in the décor. Everything was light gray, black, and white. The furniture was all black from the sofa, chairs, and desk. The sofa had white and gray throw pillows, and his desk sat on top of a white, shaggy rug. The light gray walls were bare, all except for the one behind his desk. That one in particular held three large off guard photos of Breeland and me in black and white. Looking at the pictures, I smiled, wishing like hell that we could go back to the way that we were. But… shit happens.

No longer than five minutes later, I heard the door open and close along with the clicking sound that the lock made. He was soon in view, standing in front of me smirking down into my face.

"Talk," he said, like he was just that cool. I went to open my mouth to get a few things off of my chest, but was halted when I felt his lips on mine and soon after his tongue down my throat.

I wanted to scream and shout and tell him to get off me, but I couldn't. I wanted to tell him what I was here for, how I want him to be in the baby's early stages of life, but the kiss was too damn good. I couldn't stop him.

"Why are you playing with me, Channy? You know I need you, Ma. Breeland and the baby want their mommy back at home." he said so smoothly against my lips that my legs took on a mind of their own and decided to open up a bit. Seeing that, Henny began his attack on my mouth, down my neck, and soon after came his tongue on my collar bone. Again, my legs opened a little more, prepared for whatever he was about to give. "That's right, baby, let your body say what your mouth is too afraid to speak."

"Mmm," I let out a soft moan, when I felt his rough hands underneath my shirt fumbling with my nipples. It was like I was intoxicated, straight under the influence. I couldn't stop him at this point even if I wanted to.

I lifted my ass off of the plush leather sitting chair that I was in to help Hendrix pull my bottoms and panties down. He didn't bother to take them all the way off.

Instead, he lifted my legs in the air like a baby getting ready

to get its pamper changed with my jeans and underwear

resting at my ankles. With no holding back, he went in head

first licking up and down my slit like he was trying to find a

hidden treasure.

"Damn, I've been fantasizing about eating this pussy

for the past ten days,"

His thick, slopping wet tongue parted my southern

lips and dipped into my honey pot. Flicking his tongue

back and forth, he brought it back up to wrap his lips

around my clit.

"Ahh, baby!" I moaned. I wrapped my arms around

the back of my thighs so that I could hold my legs up for

him. I watched on in pure ecstasy as he pulled back and

looked down at my vagina like it was a Vincent Van Gogh painting. "Henny, please!" I called out in desperation. I began to buck my hips so that my pussy could meet his face.

"As always, your wish is my command." He placed is face directly in front of my pussy and began to blow on my sensitive flesh. The wetness mixed with the coolness of his breath had my nub throbbing. He allowed spit to trickle from his mouth and onto my pearl. I felt as it slid down my split and to the crack of my ass. "Damn, now would you look at that?" he said in fascination. Starting from my asshole, Henny licked up his trail of saliva mixed with my juices stopping at my opening. He began to tongue fuck me viscously while rubbing the palm of his hand in a circular motion on my clit. That was it; I was outta here!

"Ahh… Oh, fuck!" I panted. My head was spinning, my heart rate picked up, and I broke out into a sweat as my spine went rigid in my seat. "Hennn… drixxxx!!! Yesss! Daddy, I'm goinggg… no, no I'm cumminnn!" Words got caught up, and I honestly couldn't tell him whether I was going or coming. Henny had that effect on me like I was sure he did with all the other woman he messed around with.

As I came down from my blissful high, it was as if my common sense was returning too.

KNOCK, KNOCK!! "Ayo, Hen Dog, we got a problem that needs your attention. It's some rowdy old man out here tripping the fuck out about his old Cady!"

Thank God! I thought. This was just what I needed; a distraction.

"Stay right here baby girl, and don't move." Henny said softly, while helping me to my feet and helping me get myself together. He placed a tender kiss on my forehead, and I savored the feel, because I knew that it would be a couple of forevers before I felt those plump, juicy, wet lips of his.

I nodded and watched as he went to the door of his office and paused. He fixed the humongous buldge that was in his pants, and I caught myself swallowing hard. *Damn, I wanted some daddy dick.* Henny turned and gave me a wink followed by cocky smile before exiting the room. I shook my head trying to get my bearings together. Once I felt that he was no longer in the hallway, I took my chance to make a quit exit. I had to get out of here. I made a mental note to never be with Hendrix alone again. I would

not be weak for this man.

Chapter 9. ZaNoni

"Mmm… Ju! That's it right there." I moaned on the verge of explosion. My hips began to buck off of the bed, and my eyes were rolling back. Right when I was about to release the stress that I had been under, he dropped my foot and began cracking up laughing. "What the fuck, Collins! Don't stop!" I whined, trying to place my foot back into his hands. The massage was feeling damn good and was exactly what I needed.

"Hush girl, ain't shit making you come but this dick." he said, as he bit his bottom lip and grabbed himself. A soft moan escaped my lips looking at my ripped up, tatted baby. I loved when he got all gangsta on me. He reached for me to come to him, and I wasted no time complying. I was ready to receive whatever it was that daddy was offering.

Before I could even position myself on his lap, the door bell sounded followed by a series of loud knocks. I was going to ignore it and pray that Ju was as well, but what did he do? Lift me off of him and go under the mattress to grab his glock. I had no choice but to follow suit. I slipped on one of his t-shirts to cover my horny, naked frame and grabbed the small .380 from the top bedside drawer.

Together, we headed downstairs where the knocks continued, only this time we could hear yelling coming from a mad man whose screams sounded almost like sobs. *No this nigga ain't,* were my thoughts before Ju snatched the door open and in walked the Hulk.

"Where the fuck is she!?" he seethed, as he began doing a sweep through our house.

"Nigga, she ain't here!" Ju yelled, but Henny just kept right ahead not listening. Once he realized that his search was coming up empty, he walked up to me, looking straight into my eyes like he was Beyonce' coming to snatch my soul.

"Where is she?" he asked through clenched teeth.

"She's umm... at her house. If not, then she stepped out for a minute. I'm sure she'll be back after a while." I said, trying to sound convincing. The truth was that Chandler and the girls were on their way over here and was probably about to pull up at any minute. Henny squinted his eyes at me, looking like he was searching for the lie that

I had just told. Releasing a long, shaky breath, he took a seat on the couch with his head in hands.

"I'm losing my fuckin mind, yo. I don't know how much more of this I can take, dawg. I'm tempted to say fuck her space and just kidnap her ass. How the fuck can she just up and leave me like this..." That was all I stuck around to hear. His ass was fuckin crazy, and I didn't feel bad or sorry for him.

I rushed up the stairs to Ju's and I master bedroom and found my phone on the floor next to my clothes. I ran into the bathroom and immediately dialed Rori's number.

"Hey Nons, we're on—

"Listen, Chandler's baby daddy is here, and he's in his feelings so I know that he isn't leaving anytime soon. Meet me at the Bonefish Grill. We can eat and talk there." I said out of breath from saying what I just said without

pausing.

"We'll be there in thirty." Rori said ending the call. I

breathed out a sigh of relief.

The girls were originally coming over so that we

could talk. Chand was still going through it, and though she

would never tell us, we all knew it. That's just how close we

all were to one another. We knew when the other was

going through something without them having to say a

word.

I got into the shower and just sat there letting the

water run all over my body. My hands went down to my

small baby bump, and I smiled. I couldn't believe that God

found me worthy enough to be someone's mother. I was

praying that He blessed CJ and me with a daughter. I

wanted her to be just like me. I could see us now driving Ju up the wall.

Sticking to the task at hand, I quickly washed my body and got out. I went over to the sink and began brushing my teeth and cleansing my face. When I was satisfied with my hygiene, I began to fix my curly hair that was thrown sloppily into a bun in the back of my head. I pulled my hair tie out and plugged in the new flat irons I had just purchased the day before. I sectioned my hair off and took fifteen minutes going through it. Once I was finished, I smiled at my reflection, loving every inch of what was looking back at me.

Curly, my hair stopped at my shoulders. When it was pressed, it easily cascaded down my back. Opting out of putting on makeup, I lathered my lips with my EOS ball and blew myself a kiss in the mirror. Still pressed for time, I hurried into the closet. I decided to dress down in a pair of light, stone-washed, True Religion skinny jeans and a plain red and white True Religion t-shirt. I threw on my low-top, white and red Jordan 11's and was ready to roll and rock. *Wait, or is it rock and roll?* You know what I mean. I gathered my jacket, purse, and keys, and headed out of my room.

I was now running late and was rushing when I walked straight passed CJ and Henny, who were in the living room smoking a blunt.

"Damn, if you walk out that door without saying something to me then I know for sure that your ass is as slow as everybody claims you are." I heard Ju snap. I stopped dead in my tracks.

"I'm sorry, baby; I was in such a hurry, I didn't see you. I'm… I'm… going to go check on Rori. She sounded sick on the phone earlier. I'll be back in a few." I stuttered over my words. I hated to tell a fib, but I couldn't risk dog ass Henny knowing Chand's whereabouts. I leaned down to give Ju a kiss, but he ignored it, got up from the sofa, and pulled me into a hug. It seemed as if he was squeezing the life out of me.

"Lie to me again, Nons, and I will seriously hurt you. Tell Chandler I said she needs to get her shit together because I ain't bout to have this sneaking around and lying shit." he said, before letting me go and placing a soft, tender kiss on my forehead. I nodded in full understanding. I hated lying to CJ, but if the shoe was on the other foot, I know that Chand would do it for me just as he would do it for Henny.

Regaining my composure, I gracefully made my way out of the house deciding to take Ju's navy blue Range Rover with peanut butter seats for a ride. He had just got this bad boy and gave me his spare key just like he did the other seven cars that he had. I got behind the wheel and adjusted the seat and mirrors. Plugging the AUX cord into my phone, I scanned my music for the right tune. Channeling my inner me, I settled on Brittany Spears song "Toxic" and trudged it all the way to The Bonefish Grill ready to get up with my BBFL's... *Bad Bitches for Life!*

~~~~~~~

"So what's going on?" I asked no one in particular once we were all seated. When I first got there, they were just pulling up as well. We all met at the entrance and was

seated soon after.

"Same ole, same ole with me. You all know I started

work this week at the Children's Clinic downtown, right?"

Brai asked, and we all nodded our heads and tuned into

what she was about to say. "Well, I think Chazman is

having separation problems. He's been doing my whole

shift with me. He literally comes to my job and sits out in

his car for hours. He'll leave when he has to handle

business, and afterwards, he'll come right straight back. At

first, I was flattered, but now, not so much. I had to chin

check two ghetto ass bitches at my job for tryna get down

on him." she huffed, getting mad all over again.

"So, what? You gone talk to him, right?" Brailynn

gave me a look like 'don't be silly'. Don't quite know if she

was really meaning that, because I indeed was just that…
silly.

"Girl, please. Chaz ain't stopping shit. Them hoes just going to have to learn the hard way. They may look crazy, but I am crazy. They can play with it if they wanna." she said taking a sip of the complimentary water that was at the table like she had not a care in the world. Rori, Chand, and I all looked at each other and fixed our eyes back onto Brailynn and fell out laughing.

"Bitch, your ass is deadly!" Chand said between laughs. I looked at her glowing skin and couldn't help but smile. She was wearing her pregnancy well. Where my face was pale, Chands was glowing despite her fading bruises. Where my sixteen-week baby bump protruded, Chand's… wait…

"Channy, how far along are you? You didn't call me after your appointment like you promised." I said, making a minor fuss at her. Chand was my baby, and I liked to know what was going on with her at all times.

"Y'all…" Chand let out. The waitress came up, and she paused for second so that we could order our food and drinks. Once the waiter was gone away and out of earshot, we all placed our eyes back onto Chandler.

"Continue, please." Brailynn said, encouraging her to finish.

"The appointment went well… Hendrix showed up." she said, as I let out a loud gasp and placed my hand on my chest.

"He didn't…" I let out just above a whisper. Hell, I was shocked. I had never seen a thug turn into mush over a woman. I mean, Collins loved me, there was no doubt about that, but he never lost his mind over me, I don't think.

"Yes, and he had the nerve to tell Mr. John that he couldn't see me anymore and that his nurse Lisa had to do my check-ups from now on." she said shaking her head. Rori thought that it was funny, while Brailynn sat shaking her head. I, on the other hand, was still stuck on the fact that he found her and showed up. I cleared my throat and shook off my thoughts.

"So, how's my niece?" I wanted Chand to have a daughter too so that our kids can grow up being best friends and cousins. Something like Rori and Brai.

"Turns out I'm ten weeks. We heard the heartbeat and everything. I can't believe that I'm the mother of a five-year-old and I'm about to have a newborn." she said,

with the widest smile on her face. It slowly faded, she

cleared her throat, and looked down at her nails.

"What aren't you telling us?" Brailynn questioned.

The waitress brought our food out, and I wasted no time

cutting into my steak forgetting all about saying my grace. I

was so hungry. I hadn't eaten since breakfast a few hours

ago. I looked back up to Chandler wanting to know the

secret that she was keeping.

"Once I tell you all this, you promise not to judge

me?" she asked the most stupidest question ever. Of course

we wouldn't judge her. Crack jokes, yes. Judge... hell no!

"After my appointment, I met Henny at his and CJ's

auto shop. We were supposed to talk, but it didn't quite go

down like that. To make a long story short, he ended up

eating my soul out of my body. It would have went further, but he had to tend to a customer. I used that as my cue and snuck back to my car without him knowing. He's been blowing my phone up non-stop since then, and I know that I am wrong, but dammit, my body needed that release." Shamefully, Chand lifted her head and fixed her gaze on us. I don't know about the others, but I couldn't hold it in any longer as I damn near fell out of my chair from barely being able to contain my laughter. Soon, the other girls joined in.

"Ain't nothing wrong with getting your pussy ate and then bouncing." Brailynn said, hyping the situation up.

"I'mma let him pull up, eat on this pussy, and dip," I let out remixing the infamous Young Thug song. The moment that her dirty deed left her mouth that was what came to my mind. The girls and I laughed and made jokes

at Chand's expense, who was laughing just as much as we

were.

We continued to eat and have a good time. It felt

good looking around the table at all of my girls laughing

and smiling. We all took a major blow with Chandler's

attack. The incident had all of us in a fucked up head

space. Now that word had gotten back to us that Zay was

captured, it was time for us to start planning our own get

back.

"So what's up? What we gone do bout Zay?" I said,

ready to get down and dirty. It had been a minute since we

all got down on somebody, and now it was time to remind

these fuckers who the hell we were.

"I know you got some shit planned; I'm down with whatever so tell me when and where." Brailynn said shrugging her shoulders. For Zay to have been her ex, she sure didn't give one piece of a fuck about him.

"I got the drop on his location. I overheard my father and Uncle Chen talking. They got him at the warehouse in China Town." Chandler offered. We sat and discussed what we were going to do about Zay until we all fell into a comfortable silence enjoying our meals.

"So, umm… I got engaged yesterday." Rori said, holding up the most beautiful engagement ring that my brown eyes had ever seen outside of my own. We all began to scream and cry we were so happy for our sister from another mister.

"I've always known that you would find love, because you are just too good of a person to pass up. However, I didn't know that it would happen in a matter of months. Hell, you beat me! But I am so happy for you, Rori! You deserve this, Mama!" Chand said, crying as she got up to give Rori a hug. Brai and I followed suit and spoke our congrats. Dinner resumed with plans of future weddings and babies. There was going to be a lot of celebrating going on for our crew.

We were just laughing about being able to have a wedding for every weekday this summer when something horrific caught my eye, sitting at the corner booth of the restaurant that was two tables over from where we were seated.

"Aahhh!" I screamed, as my heart dropped to the bottom of my chest.

"Noni, what the fuck is wrong with you!" Brailynn hissed, wiping her spilled wine from her blouse that my screaming caused her to waste.

"It's a Sasquatch!" I stood to my feet and yelled. Pointing to the ugly thing that was now looking back at me. Rorilynn spit her wine out sending it spraying in front of her. Her and the girls killed themselves laughing, but me, ZaNoni Grace McPherson, was about to start hyperventilating any second now.

"Girl!" Rori screeched, pulling on my arm to get me to sit back down. But I seen the beef jerky commercials, and I knew what those things were capable of. "That is Mo's flunky; ain't that bitch ugly?" she said laughing so hard that she began to cry. Brailynn was cradled in her

chair holding her stomach from laughing so hard while

Chand was trying to regulate her breathing. Her eyes were

red and teary. I finally took my seat still keeping an eye on

the funny looking creature that was now staring our way.

"How can he work under pressure like that?" I

asked, shaking my head. With someone as ugly as her, I

wouldn't be able to concentrate for thinking that she would

kidnap me and take me to her tribe.

"She has a thing for Mo, and I have a thing for

whippin bitches asses." Rori fumed. I noticed that Yetti

was up on her hind legs and moving closer to us. The only

thing that I could think about was that I had a baby to live

for and some bomb ass dick that I didn't want to part with

as I grabbed a hold of my steak knife. I was prepared to

engage in a knock out drag out with this manly bitch if she came with the shit.

"Rori, I see that you're having a good time. Where is Thrilla? Shouldn't he be here celebrating with you?" the he/she asked smartly.

"Hold up hungry bear! Don't come over here asking no questions in regards to my man trying to be slick with the shit. You know where he is; it's your job to know his every move. Make me slap some act right into your ass." Rori said standing to her feet, which in turn made Brai, Chand, and I do the same.

"Now, now settle down. I don't want any trouble. But come for me, I have bail money." she winked and tried to walk away, but my blood was boiling with anger at how she tried to play my Rori, so I did what any friend would have done. I tripped that gremlin and sent her big ass tumbling to the ground.

"Earthquake!" Chandler screamed, shaking the table. That caught the eye of everyone in earshot, and they all began screaming and ducking under the tables. The girls and I were laughing so hard we could barely breathe.

"Come on, let's go!" Rori said, quickly grabbing her purse. Brai, Chand, and I followed suit.

"Who's paying the bill?" I asked, picking up my plate. I was still quite hungry despite the shit that was going on.

"Fuck that shit; let's go." Brai said, making a quick and smooth exit. I followed behind her with my plate in tow.

Once we were all in the parking lot and standing by our cars, we kind of just hung out right there kickin shit and shootin the breeze like we didn't just cause mayhem inside the restaurant. But hey, we were known for fuckin shit up and leaving.

"What are y'all about to get into?" I questioned the girls with my fork in one hand and my plate in the other.

"I'm about to go lay it down. Bree is with Henny for the weekend, so I guess I'll work on planning something for her birthday. She'll be six next month." Chand said, smiling hard as ever looking like the proud mama that she was.

"Lil Chaz's is too. Maybe we can have a huge birthday bash for the both of them." Brai threw in. I kind of liked the idea.

"Look at y'all being the perfect step mother's." Rori joked. I ended up choking on my food, not wanting to laugh, but Rori's ass was crazy.

"Nuh uh, ain't no step about it, boo. I AM Lil' Chaz's mother. I would bat for that one! Lay down, do time all that." Brai snapped.

"I second that notion. I don't know what the fuck a stepmother is." Chand co-signed.

"Good grief, I was only playing." Rolling her eyes, Rori started the hugging fest, as we said our goodbyes and parted ways. I climbed into the truck and made my way back home.

Pulling up into my driveway, I noticed that Henny's car was gone. I got happy and started doing a little two-step in my seat, which led to me pressing harder on the gas and crashing into the garage door. I was so in shock that I just sat there with my mouth wide open and my hands at ten and two on the steering wheel.

"ZaNoni!" I heard CJ yell, but I couldn't move. I was almost afraid to. I knew that I was in big, big trouble. "How the fuck did you… get out the fuckin car!" Ju barked. With shaky hands, I unbuckled my seatbelt and reached for the handle on the car. When I opened it and went to get out, the car rolled forward and caused me to hit the car that was in front of me beyond the garage door. Apparently, I forgot to put the car in park before I tried to get out. *Crap! Now I'm in very big big trouble.*

I looked at Ju, my love, my life, and burst into tears praying that he would take it easy on me and not yell so much.

"Babe, I'm sorry. I didn't try--,"

"Nons, c'mere; stop crying, Ma," he said, soothingly, kissing me repeatedly on the crown of my head. *Got him!* I thought, as I turned the tears up a notch. "Don't do that, baby; I hate when you cry. But damn, Noni, we gotta do something Mama. This makes your third whip in two months that you done wrecked. Does Daddy need to teach his baby how to drive again?" Leaving a trail of kisses down my face leading to my neck, his arms traveled down my body and gripped my ass or lack thereof. "Bring them hips here, girl. Let's finish what was about to get started this morning." Blushing, that was the cue that he needed to get this shit poppin as he picked me up carefully and led me into the house.

Not being able to hold out for another minute, the both of us stripped right there in the foyer. I took it upon myself to assume the position up against the wall next to the grandfather clock.

"You ready for papa aren't you, Noni?" His husky breath tickled my ear and made my legs opened wider ready to receive him. I was seconds away from foaming at the mouth if he didn't hurry up and stick it in already. I looked over my shoulder, and Ju was smirking back at me.

"Say you're sorry first." he teased, as he rubbed his fat, meaty dick head up and down the slit of my pussy.

"I'm sorry, baby… I'm so sorry!" I said, well actually, cried. He wasn't playing fair at all.

"You don't even know what you're apologizing for, so that shit right there ain't even genuine."

"Then, tell me, please." I begged. This was cruel and unusual punishment. *Where was Al Sharpton when you needed him.*

"Nah, you shou--," was all I allowed him to get out before I got tired of his game and pushed his ass down onto the floor and mounted right on top of him.

With ease, I slid my wet wet down on his steel pole. I shuttered, and my toes curled until they popped.

"Damn Nons, shit!" he grunted, feeling the same damn thing that I was.

Together, we found the perfect rhythm and began to make a hit record. I balanced myself on my tippy toes and twerked on his dick effortlessly. CJ's hands roamed my upper body before going behind my back and unsnapping my bra.

"Take that shit off, and you better not stop riding this dick while you're doing it." he commanded with a slap on my ass. I let out a loud moan and did what my daddy asked of me and was now completely naked.

"Oh, Juuu… this dick feels so fucking good!" I called out feeling a hot flash shoot up my spine. In a matter of seconds, Ju was on his feet, and I still held my position, on his dick. With his arms hooked under my legs, he lifted me up and slammed me down onto his creamy dick that my pussy had juiced up.

"Fuck, girl! I been fuckin you seem like all my life and this pussy still feel good!!" he gulped. When his shoulders began to shake, I knew that he was about to cum, and I was right behind him. "Let that shit loose, Noni. I'm not stopping until--," He was cut short by my loud piercing scream. I felt my honey pouring out of its pot "Yeah, that's

right. Wet that dick up, Ma. Fuckkkk!" he groaned, as his

hot semen ran wild and rapid inside of me.

"Fuck CJ; don't ever take this dick away!" I stressed.

I was wrapped around him like ivy and had no intentions

of letting go. Our bodies were sweaty, and if anyone was to

walk into our home, they were sure to be greeted by our

love scent.

"This dick yours, Ma. Been yours for years now. If it

goes anywhere, you're going with it, and that's real." he

said, planting a kiss on my forehead. He began to move

carrying me in his arms. I noticed that he was headed

towards the stairs so I laid my head on his chest and closed

my eyes. I exhaled deeply with a big smile on my face.

Yeah, this was the life.

Chapter 10. Brailynn

"Brailynn, where is the heating pad?" Chaz yelled from upstairs in my bedroom. He was balled up under the covers, as I rummaged through my kitchen putting the finishing touches on our vegetable soup and grilled cheese sandwiches. I was on my cycle and was cramping slightly. Chazman, on the other hand, who was so in tune with my body that he too shared my menstrual symptoms monthly when I got my periods, was cramping just as much. It was always funny to see him have food cravings, mood swings that made me look as if I had the best attitude in the world, and cramps that had my baby ready to cry. Hell, he even took Midol.

Without answering him, because the heating pad was right in his face, I placed both bowls onto a dinner tray, along with our sandwiches, and two tall glasses of ginger ale to help settle our stomachs, and headed upstairs. When I entered my bedroom, it took everything in me not to burst out laughing at Chaz. He was balled up in my purple and white floral print covers. Heating pad now on high and a wet towel draped around his forehead. My baby was going through it. He hated *our* time of the month.

"Are you okay?" I asked, as I crawled into the bed and set our food in the middle of us. Chazman sat up, still managing to keep his towel in place and reached for a bowl of soup. He tasted it once, then twice before picking up his grilled cheese and dipping it into the soup. He focused on his lunch for a couple more seconds before he responded.

"All of this could be avoided for the next nine months if you'll just have my baby. I don't see why I gotta suffer with you? Never in my life have I been this in tune with a woman to the point that what she eats makes me shit. I'm starting to think that you got in touch with your roots and put some of that chicken foot on me." he said, as I spat my ginger ale clean out of my mouth. That was it; I was laughing hard as hell. Chazman was always calling himself being extra cautious around me. I was black with deep French creole roots, and there was no denying the fact that my Creole side practiced voodoo. However, my fully black mother had Hendrix and me along with Rorilynn and CJ in church every Sunday. She made sure that that part of my father's side was pretty much

nonexistent. We were brought up in the church, and she

wouldn't have wanted it any other way. Chaz placed his

bowl back onto the tray and picked up a pill bottle off of

his nightstand table. He twisted the cap and poured two

pills into his hand. When I noticed that the pills were

Midol, I reached for the bottle, and he pushed me away.

"Give me my Midol! You used it all last month!" I

yelled still reaching for the bottle.

"Get back, crazy ass girl. These shits works wonders.

Females be having all the good stuff." I mushed his head

then crawled back over to my side of the bed. I picked my

bowl of soup up and resumed eating my lunch.

"Really, Brailynn? You forgot the Rocky Road ice

cream," Chaz turned and snapped at me. "You were right

there in the kitchen. You know that's the only thing that can make me feel better." he pouted sounding like a little biotch. I wanted to laugh so bad, but I was afraid that he would burst into tears. I looked at his face looking back at me and the look of disappointment sent me over the edge. I started laughing my ass off, and when he let out a loud irritated huff, I began to laugh even harder not calming down until minutes later.

"Seriously, though, why you don't want to have my baby Brailynn?" Chaz questioned. I thought back to the conversation that the girls and I had at Chand's house. I was already needy of Chaz, and I wasn't ready to spring the commitment thing on him just yet. I didn't know how he would react to it, so I thought of some bullshit ass excuse to tell him until I figured out a way to come out with the real issue.

"I do want to have your snotty-nosed kid babe; it's just that I just graduated, and I wanted to at least start a career before I had any kids. We already have Lil Chaz, and we haven't been a couple for long. There's just so much that needs to be done first before we have a baby babe.

"Whatever; let that be the reason." he got out before his phone began to ring. He looked at the screen and let out a long sigh. I knew then that the call was from Jamiee, Chazman's baby mother. It was one of those rare days that she had Lil Chaz, because he would much rather spend all his time wherever his dad and I were.

"Ya," Chaz answered, and even a deaf man could hear that he was annoyed. He placed his phone on speaker and lied his back against the headboard.

"Lil Chaz is asking for you, and I'm not ready for him to leave just yet, so I was wondering if you could come over and have family time with us." she asked, sounding like family time was the furthest thing from her mind. I couldn't believe the nerve of this deadbeat. She had been doing slick shit like this ever since she found out that Big Chaz was in a serious relationship. He let me know from jump that she didn't want him to settle down with anybody but her, but I had a newsletter for that bitch. She fucking with the right kind of crazy.

"Yo, when have I ever kicked it with you on that level? Lil Chaz don't even fuck with you like that. I have to make him go over there," Chaz said, and that much was true. Lil Chaz threw a fit yesterday when Chaz told him that he was going over to his mother's house for the weekend. For whatever reason, he hated to be in Jamiee's presence.

"Why do you have to be so fuckin nasty towards me? I am the mother of your child! I bet, if I was that little red bitch, you would be breaking your neck for me just like you do her!" she yelled. This couldn't have been a grown ass woman on the phone. She was acting like every bit of a jealous, sixteen-year-old girl.

"What the fuck did I tell you about that disrespect shit in regards to my girl? She ain't nothing like what you have run off in the past. Fuck with her if you wanna, and I'ma let her handle your ass. That's your first and final warning. Now, put my Duke on the phone." Chaz said, referring to Lil Chaz.

In the Chinese Mafia, the Duke was always to be the Lord's right-hand man. Whenever Chao decided to give up his reign as Lord, that title would roll over to Chaz, and when Lil Chaz was old enough, he then would be the Duke of China Town. I wasn't too thrilled about that, because I treated Lil Chaz as my own child. I didn't want him to have no parts of the Chinese Mafia or even my own family's drug ring. What mother would?

"Hello, Daddy? Can you or my mama come get me? I don't know what I did to deserve this punishment, but I promise, if you tell me, I won't do it again. I hate it over here. All Jamiee's stanky ass talks about is you or my mama.

She only cares if you want her; she don't care about me." I heard my little man say.

My heart went out to him, because I knew that he just wanted that motherly love that Jamiee refused to give him unless Chazman was involved. That's why I had no problems with him calling me his mother and me acting like it. Lil Chaz was a good kid; he always did what I told him whether he wanted to or not, and he held me high up on a pedestal just like his father did.

"Get your stuff together; I'm about to come scoop you." Chaz said, before ending the call. He sluggishly got out of the bed and went into the closet, I assumed to throw on some clothes. Five minutes later, he came out in a pair of gray sweats and a pullover gray hoodie, and on his feet, were a pair of gray, black, and neon green Nike Air Max 95.

My baby looked sick as hell, but beyond that, you could still see the beauty in him.

"When I make a move, you should be right behind me; hurry up and throw on something. We picking Lil Chaz up and coming right back to the house." Chaz said, as he sat on the edge of the bed and waited for me to get dressed. Being that we showered together earlier, I opted for a hoe bath only washing my kitty, ass, and under my arms. Then, I threw on a purple BEBE jogging suit along with my charcoal gray Jordan 9's. I combed down my deep red wrap and placed my thick hair into a ponytail at the top of my head. I stepped out of the bathroom and was ready to go. Chaz locked up the house, and we jumped into his black on chrome Cadillac Escalade in route to Jamiee's, who stayed about twenty minutes from me.

Once we got there, Lil Chaz was sitting outside on the porch with his Loui Vuitton duffle bag draped across his shoulder. Before Chazman could even put the car in park good, the front door swung open, and out walked this beautiful, dark-skinned woman dressed in nothing but a short silk robe that barely covered her ass. Her body was banging, and her long, jet black hair swung with every step that she took, all the way to the driver's side of Chaz's truck. She opened the door to his car, and I unclicked my seat belt, because that shit was so disrespectful. Jamiee had me all the way fucked up.

"So you really brought this hoe here to my house!" she yelled, sounding as if her feelings were truly hurt, but I didn't give a fuck. This bitch had some nerve. Chazman was about a millisecond off this bitch's head, but before he could say a word, I did.

"First of all, bitch! Let the muthafuckin door handle go and try that shit again." I said, as I got out of my seat and reached over Chaz. I pushed Jamiee out of the way, then closed and locked the truck door. If the bitch wanted to talk, she was going to do it with some sense.

She began banging on the window, and Chaz looked to me asking with his eyes what I wanted him to do next. I took my time answering, as I looked over my fresh manicure and thought about what to cook for dinner. The hoe was being disrespectful banging on my man shit, and it wasn't until she knocked politely that I instructed Chazman to roll the window down.

"What do you want, Jamiee?" Chaz asked, amused by the change in her attitude since she had calmed all the way down.

"How could you do this? Is this really who you're going to choose over me?" The hurt in her eyes couldn't be missed. She was pathetic to me. I would never let my ex-nigga and his new chick see me sweat. Jamiee was damn near in tears as she asked the questions in which she really didn't want to know the answers to.

"Why the fuck are questioning me like we had something going on? For the thousandth time, Jamiee, you ain't shit to me but my baby mama. I ain't fucked you in years,and we don't talk unless it's about Lil Chaz. Cut your shit, Ma, before shit gets ugly." he threatened. I guess that wasn't what that hoe wanted to hear, because she reached inside of the window opening and struck Chaz in his nose. Instantly, blood started to seep out. I couldn't get out of the car fast enough. I opened the door, and within seconds, I was on her ass along with Chaz who was slapping the bitch silly.

"Baby, watch out, I got this." I said, and commenced to tearing into this weak ass hoe. I don't know what type of women Chaz dealt with before me that allowed Jamiee to run them off, but she was quickly going to learn that I wasn't one of them.

My fist was connecting all over her face. Her eyes were swelling, Chaz had split her lip, and her nose was leaking just like how she had did my baby's.

"Get this crazy bitch off of me!" she hollered. The bitch stopped fighting and began to cry. I don't know what type of shit this was. She started the fight, but clearly couldn't take what she had dished out.

Someway, somehow, Jamiee had slipped from underneath me, and she ended up kicking me in the face. My lip began to bleed on impact. I looked up, and when I saw that Chaz was holding her and whispering something in her ear. I straight lost it. Here I was fighting his battle, and he was saving and comforting this hoe right in front of me.

"Both of y'all bitches got me fucked up. You gone let her kick me!? So y'all wanna jump?" I said, ready to rumble with both of their asses. I went to the back of Chaz's truck and grabbed the crowbar. I ran up full speed letting loose on both Chaz and Jamiee.

"Brai, chill the fuck out! You know I wouldn't do no

shit like that!" Chaz yelled, using Jamiee for protection. He

had her in front of him, and whenever I swung his way, he

used her dumb ass as a shield.

"Mama! Come on; leave them! Let's just go." Lil

Chaz said, wrapping his small arms around me. He was tall

to be eight years old, but he was thin. Bigger than when I

first met him, but still thin. I calmed down in my baby's

arms not wanting to accidently hit him. I turned around to

look at him, and it was enough to make me cry. He looked

so torn, so sad. "Fuck them; let's go." he snapped in a hard

voice. I nodded and dropped the crowbar.

Lil Chaz picked up his bag and climbed in the front

seat. I got in the driver's seat and was about to pull off until

the back door opened. I turned around and seen a bloody

and purple Big Chaz trying to climb into the back seat. I hurried and put the car in reverse and slammed on the gas. At the end of the driveway, I cut the wheel and turned the car in the direction I needed to go to head back home. I was hoping that Chaz's ass fell out but I had no such luck. He slammed the door shut, and I continued to drive.

It took me a little under ten minutes to get back to my house. The whole ride back, Chaz was constantly saying how sorry he was and was trying his hardest to explain that it was easier to snatch Jamiee up than it was me. He was saying that, if he would have pulled me off first, then she would have for sure gotten the best of me as if I didn't have a busted lip. I didn't say shit to his ass; I had no words for Chazman at all.

"Come on, Brai, you know how much you mean to me! You know I would never disrespect you like that. If Jamiee meant anything to me, then I would have never brought you around her. I don't hide shit when it comes to my relationship with her. It's all about My Duke. I stopped the fight, and that was it Brai."

"Then what were you whispering in her ear, Chazman?" I snapped at him. I really didn't want to cry, but I honestly couldn't help it. I pulled into our driveway and hopped out not waiting for his answer.

"Wait a damn minute, please!" he screamed running up behind me. I was headed towards my car because there was no way that I was about to stick around here with his ass, and I knew that he wouldn't leave to go to his house if I asked. "I didn't want Lil Chaz to hear so whispered in her ear that I would snap her fuckin neck if she ever came at

you like that again." he said pleadingly. I… I just couldn't

believe him. He was too calmed and relaxed, and for him to

be threatening her life, Jamiee was still rowdy trying to

fight.

Shaking my head at him, I walked off and got into

my car. I backed out slowly making sure that I wouldn't hit

his truck when all of a sudden I heard a loud bang. I

jumped in my seat and turned around and seen Chaz on the

hood of my car staring directly at me. Rolling the window

down, I stuck my head out.

"Chaz, get the fuck off my car! It better not be a

dent in my shit!" I fussed. It seemed so much better to be

mad than sad. I was on the verge of an emotional

breakdown.

"On some real shit, you can try to pull that bullshit that Chandler on if you want to, and I swear to you that I will fuck you up, Kironda. You the first girl that I have ever loved. You can't take that away from me. All this over a bitch that I don't even fuckin want." He was pissed, beyond mad, but anyone could see the sad tears forming in his eyes. My passenger's side door opened, and Lil Chaz climbed in with his bag and secured his seatbelt. I sat and stared at Chaz and Lil Chaz sat and stared at me. I couldn't look at him, because I would for sure lose my resolve then.

"You're the only mother that I have. You love me, you take care of me, and you be on my ass a lot, but it's more than I can say that Jamiee has ever done..." his voice trailed off. I turned my head to look at him, and he picked his head up staring right back at me. When I saw my baby crying, that was it. I broke down and pulled him into my

arms. "You can't leave me." he whispered and began to cry

harder.

"Shhh, I'll never leave you." I said still crying. And I

meant every word.

Chapter 11. Hendrix

Chandler really had me around there going crazy over her ass. After she slipped out on me that day we were at my auto shop, I decided that that was enough playing with her ass. I burned her phone down that entire day, and when I didn't get an answer, I decided to put what I thought is the perfect plan into motion. I had been following her ass wherever she goes day and night. I was dying to be close to her, and this seemed as if this was the only solution to that problem. When we got back on track, it was imperative that I had a serious talk with my baby, because she wasn't hip at all to her surroundings.

"How much longer are you going to do this? She does the same shit every day besides on Wednesdays, and when she has Breeland." my partner in crime and current pain in the ass whined.

"Damn, nigga! Your girl at home. If it was you, I would do it for you!"

"Nigga, you a lie, and she left me!" he bolted out the last part quietly like it pained him to even speak those words, and I understood to the fullest where he was coming from. To this day, I refused to believe that Chand and I were over.

"What you mean she left? What the fuck did you do?" I spat, ready to be the protector that I had always been over my other half.

"Daddy, I'm hungry!" Breeland yelled from the backseat.

"Yeah nigga, we hungry. Stop up here at Burger King. They got their nuggets for a buck forty-nine." he said ignoring my question.

"Yuck, Uncle Chazzy, you eat those?" Lil Bit held her nose like she was really disgusted. Chaz turned around in his seat on the passenger's side ready to argue with her.

"Yeah, I like them. Don't tell me that you're a clown fan." He teased, referring to Ronald McDonald.

"I like McDonalds!" Bree snapped, with her brow hiked up. *Damn, she act just like Chand.* "My mommy takes me whenever I want." she bragged. I couldn't do nothing but chuckle. She was always throwing her mother into the equation.

"Alright, you and your mommy keep eating that shit. Your little brother or sister going to come out with one arm and no toes." Chaz said, turning around in his seat. I looked at his ass like 'really nigga'.

"Daddy!" Lil Bit began to panic and cry. Chaz turned to look at me and shrugged his shoulder carelessly.

"Why would your crazy ass say that? I swear you ain't got no sense sometimes. Baby girl, Uncle Chaz didn't mean it." I tried to reason with her, but she only continued to cry. I was ready to fight Chaz for this shit.

"While you're looking at me, you need to be looking at her!" Chaz said, pointing at the direction of Chand's apartment door. I got Lil Bit quiet and turned around just in time to see her walk out of her house and head towards her car.

Damn, my baby was looking so beautiful. I was really digging the hell out of the short hair that she was rocking. I watched how her hips swayed as she walked, and I had to readjust myself in my pants. I ain't had no pussy since this shit happened, and I didn't plan on getting any until my wife decided to open her legs to me, again. Chand had me scared to even look at another bitch.

"Why the fuck she dressed like she's about to go do somebody," Chaz asked with a frown upon his. Channy was dressed in all black from head to toe. She rocked a fitted black turtleneck that was tucked inside a pair of black jeans that fit like a second layer of skin. The only color that could be seen in her attire, were the red on the soles of her Louboutin booties. What really had me puzzled about where she was going, though, was the fact that she didn't have on any jewelry. Chandler accessorized all of her outfits to a T. Hell, she even wore studs to bed and now, going out, her ears were bare.

"Aye, what if she's going to see a nigga?" Chaz asked. I looked over at him ready to go off. I paused when I saw him crunching on my baby's Goldfish that I had packed her for a snack.

"Why you eating my baby's shit?" I snapped at this fool.

"We hungry, Daddy. Besides, he traded me." I looked back in the back seat to see that Breeland had a big bag of hot Cheetos and was having a hard time eating them. Her face was red, and her eyes and nose were running due to the fact that the chips were so hot. I looked at Chaz wishing like hell he wasn't my wife's brother. I was ready to seriously fuck him up.

"I'mma make sure my sister doesn't get pregnant for you." I lashed. I turned in my seat and took the chips from Bree. I wiped her face then hands with a wet wipe and went into her bag that I packed to get her the Kool-aid that I had placed in a travel cup. She hated the ghetto juice, but this was all we had at the house. I handed it to her, and she wasted no time giving her mouth some relief.

"Let her not have my baby because of some shit that you said, and I'mma tell my sister to never give you another chance and to move on with somebody who is more deserving of her." Chaz countered. My head snapped up towards him. We sat five minutes straight having a stare off until Bree broke the silence.

"Look, there goes Auntie B!" she said, pointing her little finger towards the doorway of Chand's apartment. Sure enough, Brailynn stood at the door locking it. When she was finished, she walked to the passenger's side of Chand's car and got in. She too was dressed in all black wearing a jumpsuit that had a deep slit in the middle showing way too much for my liking, and apparently, Chaz's too. I looked over at my new found brother and watched as his face turned devil red. All he was missing were the pointy ears and tail.

"The fuck are they going, yo?" he stressed, running his hand through his hair.

"I don't know, but we're about to go home. You're tired of following your sister around, and you're hungry remember?" I asked, starting my car after I watched Chand start hers.

"Yo, don't fuckin play right now. We gotta see where they're going. If she's about to go fuck on another nigga, then I'm going to the pen, dawg. Straight up." he seethed. The shit was funny. I wasn't the only one going through some shit with their lady, and it felt good.

"Why are y'all fighting?" I couldn't wait to hear this shit. Chaz and Brai are so much alike that the fight was probably over something stupid.

"Mann, so I went and got Lil Chaz from Jamiee's the other day, and she was on some stupid shit so Brai checked her. She asked some shit, and I gave her the answer. She didn't like the one I gave and sprung off on me," he said, looking as stressed as the day is young. "That shit set Kironda off, and she whooped Jamiee's ass. Jamiee started hollering and crying drawing attention, so I went to break it up and pulled Jamiee from underneath Brai, and she ended up kickin her in the face busting her lip."

"So you let that hoe get one off on my sister?" I was fighting mad as my hands balled up into tight fists. I was seconds away from hitting Chaz dead in his shit if he came out of his mouth and told me some shit that I didn't want to hear.

"The fuck type nigga you and your sister think I am! I would never do no shit like that. Brailynn is my heart man. Shit don't beat normal for no one else. It pumps for Lil Chaz and my family, but Brai puts the rhythm to it. I just thought that, if I pulled Jamiee off first that she wouldn't have a chance to sneak Brai as I was holding her. I was wrong like shit and paid for it when Brai went to the back of the truck and pulled out the crowbar." I smiled at that.

I was proud as hell that Brai could handle her own. Until she met Chand, it was always me that would bang with her. I knew a lot of men were against it, but my mother died before she could teach me any better. I will

hit a bitch just like I would a nigga over my sister.

"Where was my nephew during all of this?"

"Shit, riding Brailynn's dick. I couldn't believe he

turned on me for her. My feelings were straight hurt. I

was almost walking in your shoes until he talked some

sense into her. She walks around the house not saying shit

to me. Only cooking for her and Lil Chaz and only

washing his and her clothes, but I don't give a fuck; she

still at home. We may sleep in separate rooms, but at least

we're still under the same roof." he said in a mocking

tone. I rolled my eyes salty as hell in my feelings and

focused on Chand's car.

She pulled out of the lot, and seconds later, I

followed behind her, close enough to keep up and far

enough back to where I could remain unnoticed since she was in the car with Brailynn. I trained her to always be aware of her surroundings and ever so often I could see her peeking in the side mirror. We were just about to hit the expressway when Chaz's business phone began to ring, and I could tell by the huff that he let out that our little mission was about to be cut short.

"Yo?" he said into the phone. "Can't this wait for a few more hours? I'm on a really important mission… alright, alright old man. We're on our way." he said then ended the call. Chaz turned to look at me, and I already knew what was up.

"Cool, let me drop Bree off then we're there." I said, making a u-turn and going in the opposite direction to Chen's house. His wife volunteered to keep Bree for a few hours tonight, and it seemed as if it came at the perfect time.

~~~~~

CRACK!

"Aaahh! Please man ple--,"

"Shut your bitch ass up! Had I known all these years that you were a pussy, I never would have fed you nigga!" Tonight was the night that I was sending my best friend straight to hell. Anyone would be in their feelings about killing someone who has been in their life since the beginning when hustling wasn't even a thought, but the love that I had for Zay was gone the moment that I learned that he had put hands on my girl. That was the biggest mistake that he could have ever made. He knew then just as well as I did that he didn't want this type of problem with me.

"I'm saying, though, brothers for li--," was all that he could let fall from his lips before I wrapped the chain around my fist and rammed it into his mouth. Blood and teeth went everywhere and I… I was satisfied.

Chao, Chaz, CJ, and I were in China Town at Chao and Chaz's dungeon where they had been keeping Zay. The moment Chao called when we were following Chandler and Brailynn, we knew that the time had come for the bastard to finally perish. So now, in a small room, free from the snakes, because I was not fuckin with them at all, were all the fellas, and we were taking turns beating this pussy like a freak bitch that be in the hood.

"Aw man, are y'all having all the fun without us?" Chao, Chaz, CJ, and my head went up at the sound of my baby's voice. Seeing her with her all black on, wood bat hanging over her right shoulder, and her left hand propped on her thick hip had me wanting to taste that pussy again. She healed well after the attack that led us here. You could never tell that, only a few weeks ago, her face was to the point of being unrecognizable.

"Kironda, what the fuck are you doing here?" Chaz fumed, when she didn't answer and only offered him a smirk. He was going to have hell dealing with her.

"Noni, what's in the bag? I know you aren't on that psycho Mexican shit again." CJ asked. The girls were on some mo' shit, true enough, but I was just happy to be in my woman's presence.

"What's good with you, Channy? Can I talk to you for a minute?" I said trying my luck.

"Nigga, you really tryna mack at a time like this?" I heard Chaz say, but I was focused on my girl.

"Not now; after this I'll give you a minute." she sassed and walked off leading the wolf pack towards Zay. I looked on as they circled around him all wearing evil smiles that began to even send chills down my spine. Dressed in all black, they were ready to take him out, and I was ready to watch so that I could have a word or two with my baby.

"Bet you weren't expecting me, were you?" Chand asked him. Zay had little to no words to say as his eyes focused on Brailynn.

"Nigga, you better fix your motherfuckin eyes before I poke them shits out! She ain't got shit for you!" Chaz yelled walking up on Zay. "Un-cuff his bitch ass; I'll kill his fuck boy ass with my bare hands."

"No, big bro. Let me have this moment." Chand said with her lip poked out. She looked sexy as fuck, and I wished I could suck on that big juicy lip of hers. Chaz nodded his head and stepped back, but he never took his eyes off of Zay. "Now, back to you." Chand said, with a sinister smile before she came down with the wooden bat wrapped with bobbed wire and went clean across Zay's head. She hit him so hard that she left him with a new smile.

"That's my fuckin princess!" Chao boasted, looking like the proud father that he was. He was so happy to see

Chand handling business that I could have sworn I saw tears of joy welling up in his eyes.

"Sis got him looking like the Joker and shit!" Chaz said, eyeing his little sister's handy work. I didn't know whether to be scared or turned on about the shit. I could have very well been in Zay's spot.

"Again!" Brailynn shouted. Her crazy ass was getting a real kick out of this.

"Brai, get the stuff!" Rori shouted to her.

"Okay, beat his ass until I come back." she said, then walked off towards the door where I noticed they had a large, oversized Gucci duffle bag. The girls continued to beat Zay's ass with the weapons of their choice.

"Okay, I got it." Brailynn announced.

"I know y'all didn't start this shit without the Queen!" All heads turned towards the door, and standing in the doorway was Mama Nae dressed in all black like the girls, along with high-top white and black Chucks on her feet.

"Damn, Mama Dee. What you here to do? Chaperone?" Chaz joked.

"No son, I'm here to put something on this nigga that I should've put on your ass a long time ago." she said, then swung her belt from around her waist.

"Get him, Mama!" Brai shouted. The girls were having too much fun with this.

Mama Nae walked towards Zay and told the girls to back up. She circled around him, and before any of us knew it, she was whippin' his ass with a belt like he was her kid and had stolen something. Zay was hollering his

ass off. The belt was thick ostrich skin, and whenever she

connected it with his body, it left a print.

"Damn, y'all used to get whoopins like that?" CJ

asked Chaz. The look on Chaz's face was hilarious. He

looked half scared to death.

"Yo, I don't know who that woman is right there.

My mother ain't never whipped my ass like that.

"Shiddd, speak for yourself. I stayed getting a

whoopin." Chand butted in.

"It's different for girls." Chao told them. He was

always sticking up for his wife, as he should've.

"Shit, I'm tired," Mama Nae huffed, out of breath, five minutes after beating Zay's ass. "He's all yours." she said then winked at Brai and Chand.

"Oxygen is that way." Chaz cracked, pointing to the door of the room. We all held our laugh in, not daring to catch the lashing of Mama Nae's belt.

"Get your ass whooped." Mama Nae retorted, pointing her belt towards him. Chaz hurriedly shook his head no. He already knew the business.

"Noni, what you got for us?" Chand asked, walking back over to Zay's battered and weak body. Noni wasted no time going inside of a black duffle bag she had thrown over her shoulder and pulling out four cans of air freshener and four utility lighters.

"The fuck you bout to do with that?" CJ asked, amused by his girl's antics. I would be lying if I said that I wasn't interested to see what was about to go down myself.

"Are you serious right now?" Brailynn asked Noni. Chand was smiling and shaking her head before she burst into laughter.

"Spray on three." Noni told them.

"Wait, give me the purple can; it's my favorite color, and I like how good it smells." Rori said, holding her can of air freshener out for Brailynn to take.

"Seriously, I wanted this one." Brai whined back.

"Please, Brai"

"Focus!" Chand snapped. The both of them immediately switched cans and got back to the task at hand. Seeing Chand like this brought on a whole new level of sexiness, and for this to be her first body, baby girl wasn't scared at all. She was ready to handle hers and was making daddy proud in the process.

"One…" Noni started the count off. And the girls flicked their lighters on holding them a few inches away from Zay's body.

"Three," Rori finished, and the girls began to spray the air freshener onto the fire sending Zay's body up in flames.

"These folks, real deal started a campfire and shit." Chaz said, smiling on at the damage that was being done.

I nodded my head and watched as Zay began to scream and cry like the bitch nigga that he was.

"Drench him, Brai!" Chand demanded when they stopped their makeshift blowtorch torture. Zay's ass was passed out. Brailynn picked up the bottle that she placed at her feet when Mama Nae had walked in. It wasn't until she untwisted the top and poured the contents onto Zay's body did I realize that it was ammonia. Zay screamed to the top of his lungs sounding like a straight pansy.

"That muthafucka stankin'!" CJ said, fanning his nose. Mama Nae walked up and smacked him upside his head.

"Y'all need to watch your mouths around me." She fussed.

"Yes ma'am." he said, rubbing his head where she hit him at. Chaz laughed, causing Mama Nae to cut her eyes at him. He hurried to straighten his face. I shook my head wanting to laugh badly.

"Chazzy, let me see your gun." Chand said, walking up to her brother.

"Why Cheddar Bob? So you can shoot yourself in the leg with it?" he mocked. I didn't want to, but I couldn't help but laugh at his crazy ass. Chand mugged me, and I cleared my throat ceasing all laughter.

"Just give it here." she hissed through clenched teeth. Chaz sucked his teeth, handing her his gold chrome Desert Eagle, then Chand walked back to the circle of doom and aimed the gun straight at Zay's head.

"No! I wanna shoot him!" Brailynn whined.

"But I wanted to do it Brai." Chand whined back, stomping her foot down.

"But, But--,"

"Here, both of y'all shoot him and get this shi—I mean get this mess over with." CJ said, passing Brailynn his .9. Before she could turn around and aim, Chand had already shot Zay in the head killing him instantly without a blink of an eye.

"Bitch!" Brailynn looked at Chand incredulously before turning back to Zay and emptying the clip into his body. I knew my sis was cold with hers but damn. This was a whole new side of her that I had never seen.

The girls scattered and went to chatting away like they didn't just beat, torture, and kill a nigga. Their nonchalant attitudes were perfect for shit like this.

"Aye, Brai, come holla at me for a minute." Chaz called out to his girl. Brailynn rolled her eyes, but she took her ass to where he was standing. Rorilynn went into a corner, I assumed to call Thrilla, and Noni went to CJ, who was watching her crazy ass like a hawk. Chand was talking to Chao and Mama Nae, but fuck all of that, I needed her attention right now.

"Come here, Mama. Let me holla at you right quick." I called out to her. She looked at me with uncertainty, and it made me feel like shit. No matter what I did, or how hard I tried, none of that was good enough for her. If only she knew how this shit had changed a nigga.

"What's up? I got work in the morning, and it's already going on midnight, Hendrix." she said and crossed her arms. I bit my lip to hide my frustrations, but this girl was really trying me.

"So you really gone work in that old ass building, with them old ass people changing they old ass shitty diapers with my baby in your stomach. I don't think so."

"I have to work! I have two kids that I have to--,"

"Don't even come out of your fuckin mouth with that bullshit, Chandler! I put money into your account every fuckin' Friday! Half of everything I make goes straight to you, so don't tell me that shit! You ain't working there while pregnant, and once you have the baby, then we both can discuss if you can go back.

"You can't tell me--,"

"But I am! I'm sick of this shit that you're on. Damn, bae I fucked up! You remind me that every fuckin chance that you get, but the shit is getting old. You can't hate me no more than I hate myself. It hurts me knowing that I hurt you. I cry at night just like you do. The best thing that could have ever happened to me don't want to fuck with me no more. You have the power to turn everything around for me. The only one walking this earth that can heal my heart. Why can't you put me out of misery? Just come back home, Ma, please." I stressed. I hated how I could go from wanting to choke her evil ass to wanting to fall at her feet and beg for forgiveness.

"Just... I'll think about it okay?" she asked giving me hope. I bought it, but I also had something else up my sleeve to help her out a bit.

"Bree is planning a big tea party and are inviting a few friends from school. I was wondering if you and some of the girls would like to stay over and help chaperone. I promise that I will leave you alone. You won't even know that I'm there." I said, praying that she would agree. She looked at me hesitantly, and I just knew that she was going to say no.

"It's for Breeland, Mama." I said bribing her with our little princess.

"Okay, just let me know when, and I'll be there." she said and walked away. That was good enough for me. Soon, she'd be singing a different tune. I was one step closer to bringing my girl home. I just needed to get Breeland in on the plan. I'm sure about twenty bucks and a trip to Justice will do.

Chapter 12. Chao

"So, Hawaii it is. We can do our honeymoon overseas." Renee gushed, giving me a peck on my lips. I smiled seeing my world smile. That smile on her face was the highlight of my days.

Now that Zay's bitch ass was finally gone, we were planning our wedding. Truthfully, I was prepared to marry her anywhere, but when she brought up the idea of a destination wedding, I thought that it would be perfect for our family. We all could use a vacation. It seemed that, on top of dealing with Zay, all of the younger couples were

dealing with their own problems. This would be their time

to reconnect with one another and get their house in

order.

"I can't wait to be Mrs. Mengyao. It only took you

twenty-four years, babe!" Nae joked. I pulled her onto my

lap and kissed her roughly.

"Don't do it like that. The moment you came back

into my life, I was so wrapped up into loving you that I let

time get away. But let's be real Nae, you were Mrs.

Mengyao twenty-five years ago. Before you even gave me

a chance, the moment I saw you and approached your

beautiful ass in those cut-off Tommy jeans, that big

Tommy shirt tucked inside of them, those thick white

socks sticking out of those icy-white K-Swiss, those

plump lips coated in red lipstick, and the most flawless
and curvy body draped in gold jewelry, you were mine…
my wife and my world from that day forward." That was
nothing but the truth. The moment I saw Renee, that was
it for me. I dropped all my hoes that day and pursued her
for a year straight.

"I love you so much, Chao. I can't thank you
enough. You have given me two beautiful children and a
life filled with happiness now that you're back. You mean
everything to me, and I can't wait to spend forever with
you." She kissed me soft and sensual, and I couldn't help
but moan.

"The hell y'all got going on in here? This like
watching mature porn." Chazman said, walking into our

bedroom uninvited and flopping his ass right at the foot of our bed, laying out like he was at his shit.

"Nigga, if you don't get your ugly ass out of here!" I was real deal pissed at him. He pulled this shit constantly when he was younger. Whenever I got ready to get some, he would always say that he needed his mother for some reason or another.

"Damn, Pops. I need to holla at my mama right quick." See what I mean? His ass too old to be a cock blocker.

"Renee, talk to your son." I mumbled mad as ever. I had to reposition Nae on my lap to conceal my weapon that had formed underneath the blankets. She was now sitting between my legs with her back to my front.

"What is it mama's baby?" she cooed. I looked on while Chaz blushed, and I couldn't help but roll my eyes. He was seriously a big fuckin baby. Nae had spoiled this boy to no end.

"Brailynn ain't trying to give me a baby, and I need you to talk some sense into her.

"Are you serious right now?" I asked, but I really wanted to burst out laughing. I could look at his face and tell that he was dead ass.

"Yo Pops, don't clown. I really need help on this. Her friends have formed a pregnancy pact, so why can't she join? Lil Chaz will be nine years old next month. I started fucki-- I mean, I was raped at that age. He would be having his own family soon. Plus, I'm getting older. I don't wanna be a grandpa daddy." I was choking off of his rape comment. I knew that was a lie and was only a cover up because Nae was right here. Overall, I understood where my boy was coming from, because I was a man. When I fell in love with Nae, I wanted nothing more than to fill her up with my babies. I only got one in before we lost time, and now it was much too late.

"Trap her." I said with a shrug of my shoulders.

"Seriously Delun! Chazman, you cannot trap that girl!"

"Why not?" Chaz and I said at the same time.

"I can't believe you two; what is the reason Brailynn is giving you as to why she is not ready to have a child right now?" she asked Chaz. He took a deep breath and looked as if he was deep in thought.

"She said some shit about how she just got out of school and that we have time later for that. Talking about we already have Lil Chaz. A bunch of bullshit if you ask me." he stated dropping his shoulders.

"Nothing that comes out your girl's mouth is bullshit. That's your problem, and your answer right there. If you paid attention to the shit that she said then you would know that she's scared. What do people do when they are afraid of something? Run from it, right? Brailynn is giving you the run around simply because she is afraid. What's going through her mind is that she either thinks that she is going to fail at being a mother because hers wasn't there to teach her how to be, or she's afraid that she'll be doing it by herself considering her past relationship.

Every person that meant something to her has hurt her, and in a way she thinks, no, she's waiting for you to do the same. You have to let her know that you will be there and that you got her through whatever. You can't just tell her that you want her to have your baby, yet y'all still live like friends that are in the "talking" stage. A man with no eyes can see the love between you two. Hell, it's so intense, raw, and real that, even I have to catch a breath when in the room with you two. Just do right by her son. In all aspects of a relationship with her, do right. She deserves it."

"So basically, do something to show her that I'm in this for the long haul?" Chaz asked. I could tell that his mind was going into overdrive trying to think of the perfect solution to this problem.

"Exactly."

"I got the perfect thing in mind." he said, rubbing

his chin and nodding his head. *Oh Lord, here it goes.*

Here and now

I promise to love faithfully, You're all I need

Here and now

I vow to be one with thee, Your love is all I need

There was little to nothing that I could do to stop

the tears from building up in my eyes. Renee had created

the perfect evening for us on the beachfront in Maui. Pale

orange and cream-colored rose petals decorated the white sand and went along with the purples, pinks, and oranges of the evening sky above us. I stood at the altar dressed in all white linen shorts and a button down short sleeve linen shirt. To the left of me stood my Duke, and to the left of him was my forever friend, Chen.

On the other side of the peonies covered arch was my beautiful daughter looking like the perfect mixture of me and my world, dressed in a white, long-flowing gown, well sundress, which was what she called it. She looked over at her pops and gave me a big grin and a wink. I smiled at her and wiped my right eye before a tear could even fall.

To the right of Chandler stood my other daughter, Brailynn. She too was dressed in a white flowing dress the same as Chand's. Smiling brightly, anyone could see why

my son was so smitten by her. She waved and took her

hand up to her mouth and tossed it towards me wildly

blowing me a kiss. She and Chandler were so much alike

that is was crazy. They both were so goofy.

I look in your eyes and there I see

What happiness really means

The love that we share makes life so sweet

Together we'll always be

This pledge of love feel so right and ooh, I need you.

Like the magnetic force that she was, Renee

commanded my attention when she stood at the end of

the short aisle, completely taking my breath away, the

moment that my eyes landed on her. Our guests which

consisted of Henny, Rori, Thrilla, CJ, Noni, and the kids began to clap, whistle, and cheer at her as she took the first step towards her forever after.

Dressed in a pearl, sequenced, white, body-fitting corset dress that stopped at her calf muscles showcasing her curves, Renee was just as gorgeous as she was the day I met her, if not more. One bare foot in front of the other, she made her way towards me. Her hair flowed in the light breeze, and her eyes twinkled the whole while she made her journey. I couldn't hold it in any longer. The moment she stopped in front of me and flashed that smile of hers, I couldn't help falling in love with. My ruthless mafia persona left, and the man that I became for my woman cried tears of joy. The only word that could come to my mind at the moment was, *finally*.

Nae pulled me into her arms, so I wrapped my arms around her waist and tucked my head in her neck. There, in that position, she prayed over the both of us and our union. Minutes later, we let The Officiate do what he had to do and declare us man and wife. I kissed the woman of my dreams, the love of my life, and the mother of my two kids, and felt as if I was on a high that I had no way of coming down from. This was it. Renee was me and I was her.

"Congratulations Chao and Mama Nae, but if it's not too much trouble, I would like to ask if my love, ZaNoni, would you like to get married now?" CJ said. He was down on one knee, and Noni was standing in front of him skinning and grinning while CJ held her hand and asked to make things official between the two.

I can't say that I was surprised because I wasn't. CJ was like me in many ways, which was why he and I hung out more often than Henny and I. Although Noni was a lot slower than most, he saw what he had in her and refused to pass up on it even though he was still young and had a lot more running around that he could do. He found what made him happy and quickly manned up so that he could be with her. Henny was the same way; he just had to mess up to realize it. Both of the men took different paths but came out with the same outcome.

"Go right ahead son," I said. The girls began to squeal while the men dapped their partner up. I respectively patted CJ on his back.

"Come on, baby girl, are you ready to do this?" he asked with his arms now wrapped securely around his soon-to-be bride's waist.

"I've been ready." she said smiling from ear to ear.

"Dearly beloved, we are gathered here for the second time today…" The Officiate continued on with their nuptials. The night sky had completely fallen, and the only light were the lanterns and Tiki candles surrounding us. The ambiance was pure beauty. I looked next to me, and Renee was crying once the pair said 'I do'. Loud cheering appeared a few seconds later, and then they were jumping the broom.

I looked around at everyone that was in attendance and could see that love was in the air, and it felt great being as though there was so much that I knew each of the couples had going on. If for this week only, I knew

that we would all have peace on this paradise.

Chapter 13. Collins

Since getting married to the love of my life, one would think that I would be living in total bliss. That was the case all the way up until two days ago when my phone wouldn't stop ringing and ZaNoni answered it. The caller was Lasandra, one of the lieutenants that worked two of MCP's hottest traps. She was a rough bitch, but brought us in hella money. She needed to re-up when she called and couldn't get in touch with Henny so she was trying me.

Noni saw the shit and flipped the fuck out accusing me of cheating. She whooped my ass so quick that I almost missed what happened. Now, for the past two days, Noni has been walking around giving me the silent treatment. She hasn't cooked for me, fucked me, nor has she sucked my dick, and my baby loves pleasing me. The petty shit was starting to get on my nerves. We had never argued in the past, and I be damned if we start now.

"Aye, come ride with me right quick." I said, when I walked into our bedroom. Noni was laid out in the middle of the bed sitting up slightly with pillows tucked behind her back watching *Pretty Woman*, her favorite movie. She was using her belly for a place to hold her Nutella, and a bag of Cuties oranges laid beside her. I shook my head at the sight. Since being pregnant, that's all she wanted to eat. Oranges dipped in chocolate; she even got me eating the shit.

"Noni, you don't hear me talking to you?" I asked, again, tapping her on her leg. She kicked at me.

"Touch me, again, and you'll draw back a nub." she said, without looking at me. That little ass threat fell on deaf ears.

"Aye, get your ass up, yo, and stop playing with me." I mushed her head wanting to play with her, but that quickly backfired when she shot up on her feet and started swinging at me.

"Nigga, you got me fucked up! Get the fuck out my house!" she lashed. I was trying to restrain her until she said that shit. I looked into her eyes, and nothing but hurt and anger was etched on her face with a little bit of chocolate in the corner of her mouth. "Get the fuck out Collins!" she yelled again.

"I ain't going no mutherfuckin where! You mad at me about some shit that I ain't do! I have never cheated on you!" I yelled back at her crazy ass.

"Then why the fuck she still calling you?" she folded her arms and stuck her foot out. I'm not sure if this was the Mexican or black side of her coming out.

"That bitch ain't called--," I got out, before she threw something that hit me in my mouth.

"Lie again, and see how I fuck you up!" I looked down at the item she had just thrown and seen that it was my personal phone. Sure enough, Lasandra's name was all down my recent calls. *Fuck!*

"Baby, I swear it's not like that!" That was some bullshit. Lasandra only had my number for emergency situations only. I couldn't find my phone earlier, and now I know why.

"You fucked up, and now I gotta fix it." she stressed, before walking into our closet. She came out seconds later with shoes on her feet and her purse cradled in her arm. "I'll be back." she said, before walking past me and leaving. *What the fuck just happened?*

Somewhere along the time of waiting for Nons to return, I ended up falling asleep. I awoke hours later to the smell of fried chicken, and it instantly made my stomach grumble. Getting out of the bed and going downstairs, I immediately became weary and turned on at what stood before me. I sat down at the table and awaited my wife's next move.

"What the fuck!" I spat looking down at the dish that Noni had just placed in front of me. It looked like some crisped ass chicken fingers on the plate, and for two reasons I was mad. One, Noni knew better than to serve me this burnt ass shit, and two, I wasn't a child, so why the fuck was she serving me this shit. "Non, what the fuck is this?" I asked, not even ready to hear the answer. There was no way that I was about to eat this shit.

"Oh, so you don't like finger food?" she asked, looking like the devil himself dressed in a red catsuit. I looked at her big round belly and got mad as hell. Looked like she had my lil' dude hemmed the fuck up trying to fit into that shit.

"This my love… this hefty serving before you are Lasandra's fingers. I told you about having her texting your phone, and clearly you didn't take that serious when I happened to come across a message of hers asking about some 'work'. Funny thing is babe, you don't have a legal job, and I know you wouldn't inform some random about what you really do, so since my beloved husband couldn't put her in her place, I did it for you." she said with a smile as long as the Mississippi river. I, on the other hand, couldn't believe the shit that I was hearing. Did she really just chop my lieutenant's fingers off?

"Noni, please tell me that you didn't chop that girl's fingers off for real! She was texting me about work meaning drugs, not no fuckin nine to five! Yo, you grew up in one of the roughest fuckin neighborhoods. How could you not know that shit!?"

I was boiling hot right now; this was the craziest shit that I had ever been involved in. I stood from the table and began to pace the floor in front of her ditzy ass. I wanted to slap her so bad, but fuck, this was my baby. I looked up at her, and she now had an 'oh shit' look on her pretty face. It served her crazy Mexican ass right.

"I'm so sorry, baby; I didn't know. She just kept texting you, and you really didn't give me an explanation, so I just snapped and did it. I didn't know if she was trying you or not. I'll be the first to admit that this pregnancy has me a little insecure. We can take them back to her; just let me go get my purse." she said, attempting to walk off. I snatched her frail ass up. If I needed any more confirmation, that was it. My wife was slow.

"We are going to take her fingers back to her and do what with them ZaNoni? Glue them back on?" she looked at me, and I looked at her, and I knew then that those were her exact intentions. I shook my head not knowing what else to say to her and sent a text to Henny letting him know what was up. I had no doubt that, he and whoever else heard about this was going to clown me for a long as time. I turned back to Noni, and she was still staring at me.

"When have I ever given you a reason to act a fool over me since we've been together? I'll never do you dirty! You're the only fuckin woman that I have ever loved; that ring is on your finger for a reason. If even the slightest of doubt crossed my mind that I couldn't be the man that you deserve to have love you, then I wouldn't have placed it there. You gotta let this insecure bullshit go, Ma, cause I swear to you, you're all I see out here. My dick ain't jumping for these hoes, Noni, I swear." I said, shaking her by her shoulders hoping to shake some sense into her slow ass.

"You got me, and I ain't going nowhere without you, okay?" Noni nodded up and down, and I kissed her forehead. "Now, can I get some pussy, head, shit a real meal, something?" I asked, and she smiled seductively getting down on her knees. If I must be honest, this finger chopping shit just turned me all the way on. If I didn't know before, I know now that my baby loves me just as much as I love her, because I'm straight murkin behind

mine.

Chapter. 14 Chazman

"Baby, I think your dog died." I said, hating to be the bearer of bad news but not really. I was trying everything in my power to get things back right with Brai and I. It had been three weeks since that shit went down with Jamiee, and she was just now sleeping back in our bedroom at home. Desperate times called for desperate measures, and I did what I had to do. I poisoned poor little Bentley, the dog that Henny had given her as a graduation present, and just as I expected, Brailynn was distraught.

"Really? What happened to my baby?" she asked, throwing the comforter from over her body and running down stairs and into Bentley's room. I followed close behind her ready to catch her when the tears fall from her eyes. "Nooo, what happened to him!?" she asked. I cringed hating to see her cry, but I needed her more than he did.

"I don't know, babe. Maybe, he got SIDS like Noni said." I answered with a shrug. I looked down at the lifeless animal with his tongue sticking out and foam all around his mouth. Truth is, rat poisoning that mysteriously ended up in his dog food was what did it, though, I'd never tell her that. With her heart broken over her dead puppy, she would fall into my arms and cry, and I would be here to comfort her in any way possible. A shoulder to cry on is a dick to ride on, right? Shit, my dick needed to be ridden badly too.

"Chazzy, my baby is gone." she sobbed sounding so sad. I wanted so badly to tell her that we could make our own, baby, but I'd decided not to pressure her on that issue. Besides, I had something up my sleeve that would have her rewarding me a baby pretty soon. I know I may sound crazy but shit. A nigga is in love. I have never felt this feeling before, and I stopped trying to control my emotions a long time ago.

"Come on, Mama. Go upstairs and plan his funeral. I'm going to get him cleaned up and placed somewhere until we decide where and when to bury him." I said, helping my baby to her feet and semi-faking concern. I could care less about the dog. I just hated to see my woman cry. I had nightmares of her hurt face outside of Jamiee's house that day and couldn't wait for those motherfuckers to go away.

Brai nodded her head and allowed me to carry her back up to our bedroom. When we got there, it didn't surprise me that Lil Chaz was in the bed chilling on my side watching the sport's channel. He clung to Brailynn like glue, and it was like watching me and my mother all over again.

"Mama, are you okay?" he asked, when he noticed the tears that wouldn't stop falling from Brailynn's eyes. He looked at me for only a split second before focusing his attention back on Brai.

"Bentley died." she said, softly, wiping her face. Lil Chaz glared at me, and I shrugged. I knew that he knew that I was behind his death, but all I could say was that one day he'd understand. Lil Chaz pulled Brailynn in for a hug, and she hugged him back tight like she was dreading to let him go.

"It's going to be okay, Ma. I'll buy you a new puppy okay?" he asked, looking at her directly in the eyes. I stared a hole in my boy wanting so bad to say, *Go head; that fucker is gonna die too.* Instead, I rubbed Brai's back and agreed with whatever my Duke had to say. "Come on, get back in bed and take a nap. We'll plan a service for him when you get up." She nodded and got back in bed. Soon after, she was fast asleep.

~~~~~~

"Dearly beloved, we are gathered here today--,"

"Noni, this isn't a wedding. This is a funeral! I thought you said you knew what you were doing." I hissed, hating that I allowed her slow ass to talk me into doing the Eulogy at Bentley's services.

"I said that?" she said, plastering an innocent look on her face.

"Bruh, get your girl," I gritted to CJ. I honestly didn't understand how he put up with her ditzy ass.

We were all in the backyard at my parents' house having a home going service for Bentley. The guys and I dug a four-foot hole deep enough for his poor little body. The girls decorated the area of his final resting place in powder blue and white, and we all had powder blue roses to put down after the benediction. Hell, Kironda even made everybody wear all white. My baby was really down about the death of her pet, but I had something that was going to put a smile upon her face very soon.

"Since we don't have a eulogist, let's just skip to the song and then closing remarks." I said, taking my place back beside Brailynn. Noni had the radio set up on the inside so that the sound could come through the speakers outside. When the song came on starting from the chorus, I got pissed and walked back into the house. I could still hear, "Who Let the Dogs Out" by the Baha Men blasting outside, and I got even madder, but it was all my fault. I don't know why I trusted her out of everybody to pull this off.

I went into the sound room and turned the radio off. This home going celebration was officially over. When I came out of the room, I bumped into Brailynn, who surprisingly looked better than she had all day. My baby was even wearing a soft smile that made one appear across my face.

"Thank you," she whispered, wrapping her arms around my waist. I didn't say anything; I only hugged her back wrapping my arms around her shoulders. "You mean so much to me, Chaz. You go out of your way for me always, and even though these last few weeks haven't been our best, that haven't stopped you from loving me and being here now when I need you the most. I love you."

She leaned up on tiptoes and placed a kiss on my chin leaving my shit wet. I glared down at her, because she knew I hated when her ass slobbed on my face like that. Since this was a time for bereavement, I decided to

let it slide.

"I love you, girl; you ain't ever gotta trip about me

leaving. I ain't going nowhere. You got a nigga out here

insane about your mean, cute ass." I kissed her forehead,

and we went back into the living room where the repast

was being held.

Again, I let Noni put this whole shindig together, so

I wasn't surprised to see everyone in the room playing

twister. Henny and CJ were really into the shit fighting

over the last red circle. I just shook my head, poured up a

shot of Henny, and relaxed with my people. My parents

were out of state in Bora Bora for their honeymoon, and I

hated that they were going to miss the big shit that I had

planned. They would make it back in time for Breeland

and Lil Chaz's birthday bash that the ladies were putting together, so they wouldn't be out of the know for long.

Despite Noni fucking most of the service up, my big baby was now smiling, and she seemed to be having a good time. My eyes wouldn't leave her as I watched her and Lil Chaz try to do the running man challenge. When Brailynn took out running for real, I lost it. I had to hold my stomach from laughing so hard. *Yeah, despite everything, today turned out to be a good day.*

The next day, I was up and at it, showering and getting dressed before Kironda and Lil Chaz woke up. Today was the day that I was going to ask Brailynn to marry me, and there was a lot that needed to be done to make that happen. Hell, I had just gotten the ring, and that was as far as the planning had went. I hit up my sister yesterday and told her that I needed her help, and she had

me on the phone for two hours straight crying and color

scheming. I didn't know what the fuck she was talking

about. I just answered with a simple 'ok' and 'yeah' to every

other word she said to make is seem as if I was listening. I

knew without a doubt, though, if anyone could help me

plan this engagement, then it would be her.

In thirty minutes flat, I was dressed and out the door

on my way to IHOP to meet Chand since her wide ass just

had to have breakfast. When I pulled into the lot, her car

was one the first ones I noticed, because she was double

parked. For her ass to have more than one car, she couldn't

drive for shit. I found a space a couple cars over, parked

my car, then headed into the restaurant. I spotted her

immediately sitting at a window booth, and the table was covered with plates of food.

I hope you ordered something for me." I said, sitting down in front of her and observing the different breakfast platters.

"Yeah, I got you some toast." she said back, handing me a small saucer of some dried up bread. I looked at her heavy ass like she was crazy and picked up a plate of pancakes, added a little syrup, and began to eat. Chandler looked at me and rolled her eyes. "I was going to eat those, but help yourself with your greedy ass." she snapped. I reached across the table and popped her in the mouth.

"Chill out, fat mama." she gasped, and I don't if it was from me popping her or calling her fat, but either way, I wasn't about to apologize. She knew it too, which is why she picked up a piece of bacon and threw it at me. I was so shocked that her hungry ass was throwing food that I couldn't catch it and the greasy mess had hit my chin and landed on my lap. I picked it up and ate it.

"Bet you was going to eat that, too, huh?" I joked, smiling at her. She laughed it off and resumed eating her food. I loved how childish my sister and I were with each other. We picked and nagged each other all the time, and I wasn't changing that for the world.

"So how do you want to do this? Do you have the ring already? Let me see?" Chandler was hanging on the edge of her seat in anticipation, but not once did she stop eating.

"That's what you're here for; I ain't never proposed to anybody." I dug into my pocket to retrieve what I thought was the perfect ring that I had spent hours searching for. When I first saw it, I knew immediately that it was for my baby.

"AAAHHH! My bitch getting married!" Chand screamed, drawing attention our way. I blushed and gave off a light chuckle. It felt weird, but all in a good way. I met this girl, who was crazy as hell, fell in love for the first time, and though she drives me fuckin nuts, I know there is no life without her. "Damn, Chazzy! This glacier, though… this bitch is heavy!" I nodded my head in agreement.

The ring was indeed bigger than what I was looking for, but I knew Brailynn would love it. She wasn't flashy at all, but she'd show her man and family off to anyone who paid attention. This ring was something else my baby could brag about.

"What's the plan? How are we gonna get her to say yes?" I asked, slipping the ring back into my pocket. I wasn't trying to lose that pricey ice piece.

"I got the perfect idea here's what we are going to do…"

See you heard it all before, falling in and out of trust, trying to

rekindle lust,

Only to lose yourself but I won't let me lose you. I won't let us just

fade away.

After all that we've been through, I'ma show you more than I ever

could say.

The plan that Chand and I came up with was to have a scavenger hunt throughout Brailynn and I's home that would eventually led her to me, where I will be waiting in our basement down on one knee. Everything was set into place, and the house was decorated in all types of flowers, T- Candles, and lights and shit. Down in the basement, where I was placed to proposed, was a huge heart made out of red rose petals that Chand had put together, and white rose petals that spelled out the words *'marry me'*. White, red, and gold balloons hung from the ceiling along with red and white streamers that had different pictures of Lil Chaz, Brai, and myself throughout the first year that we had spent together. It looked all childish to me, but I knew my girl would love it. Brai was a sap for this kind of shit.

As I sat and waited for her to make her way to me, I listened to the music that was quietly playing in the background. It wasn't your traditional love songs or wedding music. It was actually a fuck mix that Brailynn had made for us. It was a CD with all of the songs that we had made love to on more than one occasion. When Qwote's song "In the bed" came on, a big smile came across my face.

Every time I heard this song, I started to feel giddy inside. My baby got down and did some real freaky shit to me off this joint. Before I knew it, the song was over and "Stay" began to play. I didn't know who sang it, but this was the same song that Brai had ridden my face to that night in my car after the big club fight had broken out. As a matter of fact, it seemed as if every time this song was playing, I was eating her ass out. I could smell her now. Mmm! I smiled even wider. I was so caught up in my daydream that I hadn't noticed that she and Chand were in the room until I heard light sniffles.

I looked up and there she was… hair bone straight and flat-ironed after her fresh perm. She was dressed down for the movies that she and Chand had just returned from, looking sexy as fuck in a tight tube top, white denim jeans with a slit at the knee, and a pair of white strappy Giuseppe's that she snuck and used my card to buy. It was all good, though, because I got her her own card that I planned to rack all kinds of shit up on. Teach that ass a lesson. Her green blazer sat color to her all white ensemble and made me mentally aware of how good my babe be dressing. I mean, who wears white to the movies. Brailynn muthafuckin K. is who. Her face was red, wet, and puffy from crying, but damn, did she still look beautiful. This girl was an angel. Only God's angels looked this good.

Chandler cleared her throat, and I knew that it was time for me to get this shit poppin. Wyclef Jean and Mary J. Blige's song "911" began to play, and I was feeling this shit for real. Like I said, the music was unconventional but it was us.

Swallowing my nerves, I got up from the chair that I was sitting in and walked over to my love. She was still crying, admiring the room and hadn't even noticed that I was in the room with her. I reached for her hand, and she fell into my arms crying and blowing her snot on my fresh white Armani tee. I held her a little tighter to give her a minute and whispered in her ear over and over how much I loved her, just in case she needed to hear it.

I then pulled back and got on one knee, wanting to do it the exact same way that my pops had done it for my mother, but what was shocking was that, as I kneeled,

Brailynn did too.

"You will never kneel before me. I am your equal."

she said through an airy breath. I might sound like a bitch

for this, but my heart did all kinds of crazy shit after she

said that. This woman always found ways to make me love

her more than what I did the day before. While I wasn't

shit to a lot of people, I was a king in her eyes, and that was

enough for me. I cleared my throat, because I was real deal

about to cry over that sweet shit. I grabbed her hand again

and began with my proposal the only way that I knew

how… by keeping shit all the way real with her.

"Shit, I was waiting on you to pop the question to

me, but since you was taking forever, I decided that I'll beat

you to it. They say to get something that you never had,

you have to do something that you've never done. Never have I been in love until I met you. And since then, it's like I have gained the world. I live for a whole other reason now. I see things in myself that I know wasn't there until you made it visible. Lil Chaz and I couldn't have been more blessed to have someone like you to regulate shit in our lives. Everything is not for everyone, but I know that you are for me. Life don't go on without you. With that being said, will you marry me, K.?"

I looked into my baby's eyes, and they made my own water. I was a street dude through and through, but if the woman you was fuckin with couldn't bring tears to your eyes when called for, then you was fuckin with the wrong bitch, straight up. We kneeled knee to knee, staring at each other. Brailynn nodded because she was so choked up that she couldn't answer right away. I remained still, still holding her hand waiting for her to voice her answer. When she kissed me putting all of her emotions into it, it was only then when she pulled away that I got an audible yes.

"You didn't even have to ask. Your ass was marrying me whether you wanted to or not." she said hugging me tight. I stood us up and wrapped my arms around her waist. I was feeling like a grown ass man now. My life had a new meaning and title. I was Chaz's father, and Brailynn's fiancé now.

"Shit, why you ain't ask me then?" I swatted her on her fat, juicy ass and made it jiggle. "Let me get some, so I know it's real."

"I'm still right here, you know." Chandler said, making me remember that she was still here. I honestly forgot all about her ass.

"My bad, camera man. Did you catch all of that?" I said, reaching into my pocket to retrieve her a tip. I was going to hire someone professional, but since she just had to be here, I made her work for it.

"Forty dollars! You are cheap as hell! This is the last time I'll do a favor for you." I looked at her like she was crazy. Out of all people, she called me cheap when she was the cheapest one. Her grown ass had money on top of money, because all of the men in her life, namely Henny, our father and me made sure she did. I knew she had to be close to a millionaire but was always saying how she didn't have it. Chand was the richest brokest person I knew.

"Thank you, Channy, for being here and sharing this very special day with me! I love you for life girl!" She and Brailynn hugged.

"Where's the ring?" Chand asked, making me forget that I never placed it upon Brai's finger. *Another reason why you're marrying the perfect woman.* I had gotten down on one knee, proposed to this girl and everything, and not once did she mention the ring. Most women wouldn't even accept a proposal without a ring. I reached into my pocket and pulled out the ring box. I opened it up and took the thirteen-carat, cushion cut diamond that sat on top of a silver solid platinum band. It resembled Kim Kardashians, but it was much bigger.

"Dammmnnn! Hell yeah you can have my last name, bae!" Brai said, jumping up and down. She was clapping and smiling, and I couldn't help but laugh at her ass.

"You a Mengyao now, Ma. No more of that McPherson shit." I said, giving it to her straight. I'd give my baby whatever she wanted, but that last name, I was making sure to stick to her ass.

"I can dig it!" she was so fascinated by her ring, she was looking at it the way that Chand was staring at the pancakes at IHOP this morning. "Boy, come on! I'm about to let you put a baby in me after all of this!" *Shit!* I busted out with the cabbage patch after she said that shit! At first, I figured if I proposed that this would have been the outcome, but in all actuality, I was marrying Brailynn whether we had another kid or not. I was a man that knew, when you have something good, you hold onto it.

"Lock up on your way out, Chand." I said over my shoulder. I had Brailynn in my arms carrying her bridal style. We were passing go and collecting our 200 all the way to the bedroom. It was going down tonight!

Chapter 15. Chandler

All my life I hustled just to get that mula

And stack my change up, then go see the jeweler

Standin in the kitchen I whip out that work

Standin in the kitchen I whip out that work

"Yeah, bitch! Cut up then!" The girls and I were all

at my apartment getting ready to head over to Hendrix's

house for Breeland's tea party. I was in a fairly good

mood considering all that had taken place. Since the killing of Zay, it was like my spirits had been lifted. I'd been smiling more and embracing life as a single woman with one and a half kid. Life for me was good, but there was only one thing that could make it better, but I be damned if I spoke on that though.

"Pop it Chandler!" There in my bedroom in the middle of the floor stood Rori, Brai, Noni, and I. We were all dancing our asses off, turnt up for no reason other than we were four bad ass, educated, black, independent women. I was squatting down with my hands on my knees popping my ass and winding my hips. Rori was egging me on like she always do and that only made me dance harder. I came back up, because my legs were getting tired, when all of a sudden, a bout of nausea came out of nowhere sending me flying into the bathroom

connected to my room.

"Damn, are you sure you're going to be okay?"

Brailynn asked me for only the hundredth time this

morning. Lately, I had been experiencing real bad

morning sickness and most days it kept me in bed, leaving

me no choice but to go on maternity leave early. I was

sure that Henny would be happy to know that Friday

would be my last day of work until after I had the baby

and the doctor said that I could go back. No matter what,

he seemed to always get his way.

I nodded my head at her and pulled myself up from

my resting spot in front of the toilet. I went over to the

sink, washed my face, and brushed my teeth.

Afterwards, I got into the shower and took my time under the scalding hot water, bathing myself in the sensual bath oil from Bath and Body Works. With each stroke of my face towel against my skin, I became more and more at ease about being around my baby's father. I was so over the shit between Hendrix and I. I no longer hated him. I, in fact, loved him a tad bit more for blessing me with my first child, but did I see us in the future being a couple again? No. He served only one purpose in my life, and that was to take care of his kids, which I had no doubt that he would do. As long as everything between the kids and him were copasetic, then I had no worries.

"So what are you going to put on? I don't even know what you wear to a Tea party. Do I have to dress like an old white woman? You know black people don't do tea parties. We have barbecues and cookouts, you know; shit like that." Brai asked, as soon as I stepped out of the shower. I laughed a little at her silliness and headed to my closet in my bedroom to scan and see what I could fit.

"What are Rori and Noni wearing?" I asked Brailynn, after she had followed me into the closet. I had been back at my apartment for weeks now, and she had already fallen back in her old routine using my room and bathroom as her own.

"I have no clue. I'm throwing on some jeans, a shirt, blazer, and heels. Something simple, cute and fit for any occasion." she said and I nodded. I scanned my closet and decided to wear what I could fit.

I picked up a heather gray spaghetti strapped sundress that fit every nook and cranny of my body to a T. Quickly lotioning my body down, I placed the dress on and had Brailynn assist with my accessories clasping my necklace, anklet, and bracelets.

While she went to the bathroom to shower, I went over to my vanity to moisturize my face and touch up my hair. I had just left the beauty shop that morning, and my finger waves were soft and on point. When I was finished, I glanced in the mirror and shrugged. *That'll do.*

I was hungry, and the girls were still getting themselves together so I went into the kitchen to see what I could find. In the fridge, I spotted Rori's Chinese food from earlier and Brailynn's strawberry mango smoothie.

Being that we were best friends and all, I helped myself to it.

"Damn, how you know I wasn't gone eat that?" Brailynn asked, as she came down the steps and into the living room where I was seated on the couch enjoying my, well Rori's meal.

"Because, trick, it ain't yours." I said, getting ready to put a piece of orange chicken in my mouth when Brailynn took the fork and intercepted. I looked at her through evil eyes.

"Fat ass; I know you ain't mad over someone else's food." she said, staring back at me. I continued to look at her until she laughed. "Here. I'mma go get me a fork." she said handing me my fork back and taking off for the kitchen. I swear I couldn't stand her. Her ass always wanted something, but that's my baby, though. She came back and flopped down beside me, and together, we dug in and drank from the same cup… her smoothie.

"Damn, both y'all asses are in violation!" Rori yelled, when she saw that Brailynn's greedy ass bout ate all of her food. If I didn't know any better, I would swear that she was the one pregnant and not me.

"Chandler started it." she ratted. I made a gun with my pointer finger and thumb and stuck it to her head.

"No snitching!" she waved me off and continued to eat.

Brailynn, Rorilynn, and I were waiting on Noni so that we could go because the tea party had already started an hour ago. I was beginning to wonder what was taking her so long until she came down the steps in a huge royal blue 18ᵗʰ century styled dress. I was the first one to see her because of where I was sitting, and I could do nothing to hold my laugh in. All I could see was her head. I was cracking the hell up at my girl. When she came around the corner and in full view for Rori and Brai to see, they lost it. We were hollering, screaming, and laughing all in one.

"Look, she even have on the white gloves!" Brai joked, sending my stomach to hurt.

"Bihhh, where my phone? Her ass going on social media!" Rori said, getting up off of the floor and searching for her iPhone.

"You bitches are underdressed; this is a tea party we're headed to." Noni explained.

"Noni--,"

"You shall call me Brittany, Mademoiselle." she corrected in her fake British accent sending us into another laughing fit. I promise I wouldn't trade nan one of my girls for the world. When I say that there is never a dull moment with us, I mean just that... never.

~~~~~

"Why the fuck she keep looking over here?" I lashed. The tea party was in full effect. Breeland was dressed in her princess Belle costume and her friends, Tiara and Morgan were dressed similarly, in Cinderella and Rapunzel costumes. Tiara's mother was being extra friendly with Hendrix, and I knew that the bitch was trying to make me mad, because every time that she talked and touch him, whether it be his arm or hand, she would look at me. If only she knew that she is barking up the wrong tree, because belly or not, I would straight drag her ass.

"I don't know, but she can get her issue if she wanna." Brailynn huffed. She peeped the shit before I did and was ready to pop shit off. Two things were wrong though. There were kids in the house for one, and two, Henny no longer belonged to me. Boy, did I not like this shit.

"Fuck her! That hoe think she doing something. He ain't even paying her ass any attention. He too busy following you around and watching you out of the corner of his eye." Rori said, trying to make me feel better.

"That's true; when you went to the bathroom, he was standing at the end of the hall peeking around the corner like a crazy person." Brailynn snitched on him. I couldn't help the blush that I know appeared across my face. There was no secret that I loved Henny, and I missed his ass more than anything, but the shit he did fucked it all up for us for real. I'm a strong woman and can put up with a lot, but that cheating shit is dead. There were too many diseases going around for him to be playing with my life like that.

"Where's Noni at?" I asked, getting off the subject. She had been missing in action for about fifteen minutes now, and being that she was pregnant and had that big ass dress on, I wanted to make sure that she was okay. As soon as I got out of my chair to go look for her, her dressed stepped around the corner, and seconds later, her body was in view.

"Hahaha! Why the fuck would you let her wear that?" I heard Shaw, Tiara's mom, say. I looked up, and she had her phone out like she was recording Noni. *Hell naw! Not my baby!*

"Bitch, you got a problem?" Brailynn beat me to the punch.

"Nah, ain't no problem, but y'all can't be real friends if you let your home girl walk out the house like that. This may be a tea party, but we still black." she sassed.

"And where were your friends to tell you that you shouldn't come out with a face like that. My dog, God rests his soul, looked better than you with his overbite and all. Get you some business before you step in something that you can't get out of." I guess Brailynn pissed her off, because she began taking off her earrings, and where we were from, that meant that you were preparing to throw down. Wrong move. Before she could even get into her fighting stance, I was on her ass taking out some much-needed frustrations.

"Get the fuck back, Chand! Henny!" I heard Brailynn call before I was pulled back, and she was now in, fucking Shaw's head up.

"You was really fighting while my baby up in you?" Henny whispered in my ear, and I could tell that he was pissed, but he was loving being this close up on me. I could feel it in his jeans.

"Let me at this bitch." Noni said, trying her hardest to scrap in her dress. I wanted to laugh, bad, but now wasn't the time. Rorilynn finally broke the fight up after she had gotten a few punches in and dragged Shaw out of the house. Seconds later, Rori came back in only to leave

back out with Tiara in tow. That was is it; the tea party

was over. I was feeling bad for messing up my baby girl's

night, but she wasn't upset at all.

"Mommy, can you show me how to fight like that?"

she asked me excitedly. She was hopping from one foot

to the other fighting the air. I had to be more careful and

mindful of what I did in front of my child.

Later on in the night, all the girls were in the theater

room watching all the movies that Lil Bit wanted to

watch, which was *Tangled* and *Beauty and The Beast* back to

back. We made pallets on the floor, popped popcorn in

the popcorn machine, and had a wide assortment of

candy and fruit. Despite the drama earlier, the night ended

perfectly, and it was time for me to wind it down said my

body, as I laid comfortably on the floor and allowed sleep to take over.

"Channy," I faintly heard my name being called.

"Lorenz, is that you?" I asked, sleepily, with a lazy grin on my face.

"Yo, who the fuck is Lorenz, Chandler?"

"Tate, Lorenz Tate. You don't know your name anymore." I heard him let out a sigh of relief, and then a wet kiss was placed upon my forehead. The sweet gesture woke me up, and when I opened my eyes, I realized that it was only Henny. I rolled my eyes at him and turned over ready to go back to sleep so that I could spend a little more time with my baby Lorenz.

"Come on, Mama; come get into bed. This floor ain't good for you and the baby." Henny whispered in my ear. I wanted to fight him on it, but damn, a bed sounded so good right now.

I got up with Hendrix's assistance, and together, we climbed the stairs of the theater to the main floor, and the main floor stairs to the bedroom… our bedroom. I wasted no time climbing into bed and settling on the side that I once claimed as mine. Minutes later, I was sound asleep.

SLURRRP! GRRR, SLURRRRP!

I was awakened by a wet feeling between my legs and sounds of a hungry animal feasting and growling at his dinner.

"Mmm, shit!" I moaned, as a flame of want and desire shot through my body. I opened my eyes, threw the covers back, and was eye to eye with Henny down between my legs. My spine shook, and my head fell backwards; his tongue was feeling so fuckin good. I began to grind my pussy against his mouth, while he continued to lick up my juices.

"Fuck," he spat, when my legs began to shake. My back arched shoving more of my kitty into his face. Like the good fella that he was, he took me into his mouth and began sucking on my clit. I released a load groan and wrapped my legs around his head. I was squirting, and it was running out of me like an overflowing tub of water.

"Oooh-wee, look at that pussy pumping." Henny whispered, like he was awestruck by what only he could make this pussy do. "Turn around, Mama." he said, lifting up and giving me room to obey his orders. I did, lazily rolling over onto my stomach, bracing myself on all fours. The orgasm that he had just given me had me beyond sleepy, but he wasn't ready to stop. He latched his mouth onto my clit, and again, I could feel my pussy hopping in his mouth. When I felt his long, thick finger penetrate me, I called out his name, and began to fuck it like I hadn't had dick in a while, because shit, I hadn't.

"Oh, baby! Fuck! Just like that." I moaned, throwing my ass back. Henny continued to work his fingers and suck on my clit. I felt my temperature rise and another orgasm was on the brink. I bit my bottom lip and tightened my walls around his fingers, leaving them at my mercy until he withdrew them all too soon. "Why'd you fuckin stop?" I asked gasping for air. My body was tingling, and if Henny was to even blow on me, then I was sure I'd come off his breath alone.

"Shut the fuck up, and turn over," he commanded. I turned over, not needing to be told twice, and spread my legs eagle style. Finishing what he started, I stuck my middle and ring finger into my mouth, and then, inserted them into my love hole. I shuddered at the feeling and began to rotate my hips in a circular motion. With my free hand, I took hold of my nipple and pinched it slightly. Since being pregnant, my breast had become very sensitive, and my pinching on it was sending me up the wall.

"You putting on a show for daddy?" Henny asked. I looked into his eyes and got lost. He stood at the foot of the bed with his thick heavy dick in his hand stroking it up and down. My baby daddy was looking so fuckin sexy that I couldn't help but to come, hard.

"Move your hand. It's time I come home." he whispered. Climbing onto the bed, Henny made his way between my legs and on top of me. I held my legs up in the air while he pushed his way inside of his secret place. "Damnnn!" he moaned, and I could feel my pussy cream just by the way his deep voice sounded full of pleasure. Henny was right; this was home. For hours we fucked, kissed, talked, and made love until we fell off to sleep.

The sun shining into his bedroom the next morning was what had awoken me and my senses. *What the fuck did I just do?* There was no denying that I loved Henny, but I'd never be able to trust him. This was a big fuckin mistake.

The sex was great, but I had to go. I quietly got out of bed not wanting to wake him up and slipped on my clothes. Leaving out of the bedroom and the house unnoticed, I got into my car and peeled off. I dipped out on Hendrix, again.

CRASH!

I looked outside of my living rooms window and was ready to jump out of it. I couldn't believe what I was seeing. Henny was outside on some Jasmine Sullivan shit busting the windows out of my car, and it looked as if my tires were on flat by the way my car was leaning on one side. I wanted to cry, because I bought that car with my own money and paid the note on it until Hendrix brought it upon himself to pay it off. I loved my baby Nissan.

I came back to reality when I saw him jump on the hood and start stomping on my windshield with his heavy ass foot covered in Timberland boots. That right there let me know that he meant business, because it was hot as shit outside. Two kicks was all it took for the glass to go crashing into my front seats. I hurried and slipped my feet into my PINK slides and rushed out of the house and to my vehicle where he was now ripping off my side mirror.

"What the fuck is wrong with you? How could you do this?" I was now crying viewing the damage. My shit was all fucked up. I didn't even want it anymore. I looked at it once more. Hell, even if I did, it was totaled now.

"You wasn't supposed to leave, Chandler. Where the fuck you think you going when I love you! I've been playing by your rules all this time, but I see you have yet to get off of that dumb shit. Go get in the fuckin car, and don't ask me shit else!" Henny had this crazed look in his eyes showing so many emotions behind it. Love, hurt, and tiredness, maybe, but I couldn't give a fuck less. It was because of him that we were in this space.

"Why the fuck would I do that? Look what you just did to my car!" I yelled. *This shit is unbelievable,* I thought, shaking my head. Henny looked at me and started to make his way towards me. The expression on his face had me changing my defiant ways with the quickness. I started speed walking to his truck and made it there before he could reach me. I climbed into the front seat hating that he had just punked me out, but I wasn't about to bump with his wild, crazy ass.

Five minutes later, Henny came out of my house with my purse in his hand. He got into the car and placed my bag on my lap. Not saying a word, he sped off, tires screaming for help, and made his way out of my condominiums.

"Henny, I'm not ready to go back to your home." I heard myself say after riding a few minutes in silence. This man was so pissed, I was sure that I could fry an egg on his head.

"Henny."

Silence.

"Hendri--,"

"Chandler, please shut the fuck up right now. You only got one other option, and I'm taking you to it right now." I didn't like how that sounded one bit. I sat back and looked out of the window not saying anything else. Either this nigga was crazy or in love. My mother always told me that a man becomes a different version of himself when his heart is involved. I knew that Henny loved me, but the shit he did had me looking at him sideways. I needed trust in a relationship; it's just how I function. I didn't want to always have to worry about where my man was, who he was with, what he was doing, and shit like that. I wanted to be at peace knowing that my man could sit in a room full of bad bitches, and them hoes wouldn't get a second glance from him. *Fuckin' Henny!*

Thirty minutes of more silence, we pulled up to this modest building that was connected to a funeral home.

An uneasy feeling crept over me, and I was really beginning to look at this nigga funny now.

"What are we doing here? Did someone die?" I asked in one shaky breath.

"Nah, ain't nobody die yet." was all he said before he got out of the car and came over to my side. His rude ass didn't even attempt to open the door. He just stood off to the side with an impatient look on his face as if he was telling me to hurry up. Since I was scared of his ass at the moment, I wasted no time getting out of the car on weary limbs and took my place next to him before he took off making his way into the building. I followed suit, following close behind him. When we walked past the receptionist desk and into a room full of caskets, I became spooked as hell stopping dead in my tracks. I felt my

hands begin to shake as my anxiety levels went up.

"Pick one Chandler. If you want to leave me, this is

the only way that you can go." I gulped hard. *Aw shit!*

Chapter 16. Rorilynn

Damn, girl. You did it all in one year. Found a man, fell in love, got engaged, and now you're pregnant…

"But a baby though…"

You are nothing like your mother. Stop worrying. You are going to be just fine.

"But how will Mo feel?"

I was literally going back and forth with myself about the news that I had just discovered. After being sick for the past three days, and googling my symptoms, I came to the conclusion that, either I was pregnant, or I had stomach cancer. Being in total fear of both, I scheduled the earliest appointment that I could with my doctor for seven in the morning, but being pregnant was something I could find out right then, so a trip to Walgreens was all it took. Three tests and a 2-liter of Pepsi later, and I was one shocked mama. For real. Now all I could think about was the little life inside of me, and if I was going to be a single parent or a happily married wife and mother. Mo and I never mentioned kids to one another, but did that mean that he didn't want any?

I was at our new house cleaning things that didn't need to be cleaned, but that was just something that I did when I had a lot on my mind. I was scared shitless to tell Mo that I had gotten a positive pregnancy test. Marriage was one thing, but a baby for me was something totally different that caused more responsibility. Marriage was about fighting, because I forgot to grab milk from the grocery store. Having baby was a whole life that I was going to be responsible for. Thinking about it, maybe it's not his reaction I'm afraid of. Maybe it's me; I'm afraid of being a mother, because my own was shitty. *Ugh, this is too much.*

Needing to hear his voice, I placed the unfolded shirt I had in my hands and went to get my phone, so that I could call and check up on him. I would tell him about the pregnancy at another date and time, but I was dying to hear my baby's voice.

I flopped down on the bed in our bedroom and went to find Mo's name in my phone. Coming across his number, I tapped it and placed it on speaker phone. When his phone rang twice, then went to his voicemail, I sat up in bed a little and dialed it again, only for it to do the same thing. Trying my luck one more time, I dialed his number for the third time.

Let me lick you up and down, til you say stop

Let me play with your body baby make you real hot

Let me do all the things you want me to do

Because tonight baby, I wanna get freaky with you

I was greeted by loud music blaring through my phone. The shit was so loud that I had to cut my volume down.

"Moriah!" I yelled, trying to get his attention, but the voice that responded was not the one that I was expecting.

"He's busy right now; I'll give him back to you later." that out of order face hoe Jackie said into the phone. My body got extra hot, and my hands began to shake. *Aw, hell naw!*

"Listen here, you bitch--," I was instantly cut off by Mo's voice in the background.

"Aye, Jackie, come here for a minute!" I heard him say over the loud music and other voices that could be heard.

"Sorry, *we* can't chat right now!" she said before hanging up. I tried to call his phone again, and it didn't even ring this time. Just went straight to his voicemail. *They done fucked with the wrong one!*

These bitches had me so fucked up, and I was about to show them just how much. I hopped out of the bed, went into my closet, and threw on a pair of sweatpants and a t-shirt. I stuck my bare feet inside of my Air Max and wrapped my hair up in my scarf. I then went into my bathroom and grabbed the jar of Vaseline that was under the sink and rubbed some on my face. I was ready to kick some ass.

I rushed to my phone to call the one person that I knew would have my back, right or wrong, pregnant or not. She picked up on the second ring, smacking into the phone. Her ass was always eating.

"Put the plate down and get dressed; I need you to ride out with me right quick." I grabbed my keys and wallet out my purse before turning the lights off and heading into the garage.

"If I ride with you, you gotta promise to take me to McDonald's afterwards." she breathed into the phone. I sucked my teeth.

"Bitch, ain't you eating now?"

"Do you agree or not?" she sassed. I rolled my eyes.

"Be ready in five minutes, Chandler." I hung up the phone, jumped in the Jeep, and plugged my phone up to the radio. I specifically played Mya's song "Ridin" because that was the exact mood that I was in.

Five minutes later, I pulled up in front of Chand's house, and I didn't even have to blow the horn. Chand and Lil Bit came straight out looking like they were dressed for bed with their pajamas on, but they both had on sneakers.

"Who you about to beat up Cousin Rori?" Lil Bit asked after I pulled off.

"This ugly bi--," I started to say but was cut off.

"Nobody, girl. Hush and sit back." Chand said laughing. I looked at her and shook my head. My road dawg was looking real content with a big ass jar of Skippy peanut butter and a plastic bag full of celery slices. She even had a silver butter knife from the house to help assist with her snack.

"Give me one." I said, reaching my head over for her to place the food into my mouth since I was driving. I ate it and Chand wiped the corners of my mouth. I winked at her when she finished, and we both burst out laughing.

"That's why Uncle Chazzy said that yall were gay." Lil Bit said; I began to choke off my laughter. I swear, I couldn't stand Chaz and loved him at the same time.

"I'ma kill Chaz's ass. He know better than to say some stuff like that to you. Ain't nobody gay. You too young to even know what gay means." Chand fussed. I looked in the rearview mirror at Breeland, and she was sitting back smiling like 'yeah, whatever.' I shook my head, and at that moment, I decided not to ever leave my child with Chaz.

We rode around for two hours listening to the same song on repeat and trying to find where the hell Thrilla and Thunda Twin could be. I rode by all of OUR properties, since he had added my names to the deeds. I drove past the nightclubs and lounges that he visited. Hell, I even rode past Jackie's small town home. It wasn't until I pulled into the Shell gas station that I had some luck. Right when I was about to get out and pump the gas, Mo's white and black R8 Spyder drove by and parked at the pump in front of us. He didn't even notice his own car when he drove past.

"Duck down, and be quiet." I whispered to Chand and Bree's little ass since she wanted to tag along. We watched as Mo got out the car and went into the store. At the same time, Jackie's ugly ass got out of the car to throw something away and climbed right back in. "So this is how they wanna do it?" I began to talk to myself. "Okay, okay. Let's play then muthafuckas." I twisted my neck from side to side loosening up and getting the kinks out. I turned to Chand and caught an idea.

"Let me see your knife." I said with my hand stretched out towards her, but my eyes were back posted on the car and the door leading into the store.

"What, bitch? I'm eating." she said like it was going to kill her to let me utilize it.

"Give. Me. The. Knife. Please!" I said, through clenched teeth. Chand handed the butter knife over with a huff. I kissed her cheek and got out of the car.

I walked right up to Mo's Audi and climbed in the driver's seat. Jackie looked surprised at first until she saw who I was and had the nerve to roll her cocked ass eyes.

"Get the fuck out of the car bitch." I spoke calmly.

"Tuh!" that hoe had the audacity to say, then she rolled her eyes again and looked out of the passenger's side window. *Dumb ass!*

Quickly, I put the nappy headed hoe in the headlock and placed the butter knife to her throat. She began to panic but couldn't scream because I had my arm around her neck tightly just like CJ had taught me when I was younger.

"I'mma tell you again, bitch, get the fuck up out of my niggas shit before your blood be all over these butter soft seats." I spat, then pushed her ass so hard that her head hit the dashboard and bounced off of it. She quickly opened the door and got out leaving her raggedy ass purse behind. I rolled the window down and threw the cheap shit out of it and cranked the car up. What pissed me off even more was that Mo had bout a full tank. I pulled off with screeching tires, laughing at the fact that they ass didn't have a ride home. I looked in the mirror and Chand wasn't following me, which was off because I saw her pull out right when I did. I pulled my phone out and called her.

"Bitchhh! You got me and Bree Bree rolling! That girl got out and took one step before falling on her face." she said, laughing into the phone. Lil Bit was laughing so hard that she began to hiccup. I was pissed, but couldn't help but to chuckle at those two goofballs.

"Where'd y'all go? I thought you pulled off behind me?" I asked. Chand didn't say anything. I looked at my phone to see if she had hung up, and the call was still going. "Chand--,"

"Hold on, Rori. Umm yes, may I have a twenty piece nugget meal, large fry, cup of vanilla ice cream, and an apple pie... Breeland, what do you want?" I hung up the phone. Her fat ass was no good. I should have known she was headed straight towards the golden arches. I relaxed in my seat and enjoyed the quiet ride to the house.

Back at home, I was laid up under the covers sleeping good as hell. The air was blazing, and I had my fan on high. All of that was cut short when the covers were snatched off of me so hard that my scarf and one of my socks went with it.

"Get your ass up, Rorilynn!" I heard Mo yell. The way he said my name with no reference to being Mrs. Batiste had me wide awake and alert. I wanted to tell this nigga that he needed to try this shit, again, but the look in his eyes told me that it would be best to keep my mouth closed. "Why the fuck you didn't tell me that you had an issue with Jackie? All of this shit could have been avoided! Then, you leave me stranded with the hoe at a gas station an-hour-and-a-half away from the house! I don't know

what hurts the most, the fact that I lay down next to you

every night and give you this dick, yet you don't trust me,

or the fact that you left me. You jacked my fucking car

and left me with the bitch that you don't want me with! I

was supposed to leave with you!!" he roared.

I felt bad and small. He was right. Mo never gave me

a reason not to trust him, but he acted like he was blind to

the fact that Jackie liked him. Still, if he wasn't stressing it,

I shouldn't have been either. Mo was about to continue

his lecturing until his phone began to ring. Placing it on

speaker, he answered.

"Thrilla!" Jackie's voice came through on the other

end. Before she could say anything else, Mo cut her off.

"Look, Jackie. It's been real, but you're fired. I'll put in a recommendation for you, so that you can secure another job, but your time with me is up starting now. My wife ain't fuckin witcha, Ma, therefore I can't either. I hope you understand, and if you can't, then I don't know what to tell you. Be good to you." He ended the call and looked me in my eyes. "Get your mind right, Mrs. B." I nodded in agreement, and Mo went into the closet to undress before stepping into the bathroom to have his shower.

I got out of bed and followed behind him, taking my clothes off on the way. He fixed the shower water to his liking and stepped in; I got in behind him.

"I'm sorry," I whispered. I laid my head on his back and wrapped my arms around his waist.

"Shut up; you don't have to apologize. I just need you to know what you have in me. I'm a real man, and I meant what I said when I told you that I love you. I was serious when I asked you to be my wife. You gotta understand that I won't do anything to hurt you. Can't no woman take me from you, not even Halle Berry's old fine ass." he said laughing. I smacked his abs and chuckled as well.

"I'm pregnant." I revealed. I held my breath waiting for his reaction. He turned around, still in my hold, and placed his hands on my waist.

"I know. I saw the test in the trash before I woke you up." he smiled down at me. "Thank you for carrying my seed. We have to be married before he comes. I want you to give birth to my first born with you carrying my last name." I smiled up at him loving the way that he made me feel. Mo looked at me as if I were his world and everything in it. What was even more exciting was that he treated me as such. I was living in heaven on earth, and as long as these hoes fell in line, then everything would remain as perfect as it was.

Chapter 17. Brailynn

Damn, what else can I say? I have been in my own world since Chazman proposed to me a week ago. I never would have thought that I would find someone to love me as much as he did. For so long, I was considered the crazy one in my relationship, but now, I had someone who was just as crazy as me, if not more. Chaz and I were perfect for each other, and unlike when I was with Zayden's hoe ass, I knew that this was it for me. I was in love for the first time in my life, and the plan was to hold onto it forever.

"Come on, Mama. Let's go before it's time for you to meet up with your girls, and I still have to pick up the cake for the party." my baby said into my ear. I was laying on the couch dressed down in a pair of white stretch jeans, gray crochet sweater, and a pair of wheat Timbs. My hair was freshly relaxed, so I had it down in a wrap. My Fendi shades were placed over my eyes, and I was in a zone, not prepared for what Chaz and I were about to do, but the fact that he would be accompanying me was going to make the trip bearable.

I arose from my comfortable spot and looked at my babe, who was already looking at me.

"Yo, why you be staring at me like that? Every time I look at you, you always already looking at me." I asked Chaz's weird ass. He was forever staring at me, and in the beginning of our relationship, it used to creep me the hell out, but I eventually got used to it.

"Man, your ugly ass is so fuckin beautiful Brailynn. I get caught up sometimes. I can't believe that I actually bagged somebody like you. Now you bout to marry a nigga and shit. Heart be pounding every time I look at your pretty ass." he said with a shrug like it was nothing. I couldn't help but laugh as the butterflies did the whip and nay-nay in my belly.

"Let's roll; I'm ready to get this over with." I grabbed my purse and headed to the garage to choose which car of Chaz's that I'd be pushing for the day. I opted for the new Benz, grabbed the keys, and pressed the automated start button. Chaz lifted the garage by the button on the wall and swaggered to the passenger's seat. He got in and reached across the console. I was about to question him about what he was doing until I noticed that he was strapping my seat belt in for me. It was little shit like this that had me falling for him over and over again. The crazy part about all of it was that I didn't even think that Chaz knew what he was doing half of the time. This man was every woman's dream, and he was all mine.

"Why you been wearing them sunglasses like you trying to hide a black eye? People are going to think that I'm beating on you." Chaz asked, causing me to smile big. I slowly pulled out of the driveway before I answered him.

"My ring be blinded me bae. I'm like Velma; I can't see shit without my glasses." I said holding my hand up that housed my engagement ring. Chaz laughed like I was joking, but I was dead ass serious.

"Your ass is foolish." he chuckled. I smiled hearing him laugh. It was the sexiest shit that came out of his mouth besides his moaning when he's buried deep inside of me.

I cut the radio up to give us something to listen to while we took the hour and a half drive to the cemetery. Today was Saturday, and Chazman had kept his word by us going to visit my parents' grave site every Saturday morning. I always dreaded going, but I had to admit that this form of therapy was working for me. I was finally accepting that they were no longer with us and talking to them and catching them up on the happenings of Hendrix and I always left me feeling like they were still here in a way. This visit was going to be special, because I had some exciting news to tell them; it was truly going to be a bittersweet moment.

I pulled up to my regular parking spot that was right in front of the burial site and placed the car in park. I sat there for a minute and gave my heart time to slow its rate.

"Are you okay, babe?" Chaz asked. He placed his hand on my shoulder and gave it a comforting squeeze. I closed my eyes and briefly thanked God for him. I placed my hand on top of his and patted it, letting him know that I was fine. We both got out of the car, and I took the steps to the two golden headstones. I looked back towards the car, and as always, Chazman was posted by the passenger's side door puffing on his blunt. I blew him a kiss and focused back on the reason that I was here. I sat in the middle of the tombstones and took a deep breath. My father's grave was on my right and my mother's was to my left. I laid my head onto my mother's and wrapped my arm around my father's. I sat like that for a minute before I began to speak.

"Mommy, Daddy. I first want to tell you guys how much I miss you both. Life has proven to be so hard without you two. I thank you guys again for everything that you have done for Henny and I, and mom, you, for making me the woman I am today. Although I was just a teenager when you passed, I will never forget the lessons that you taught me." I took another deep breath and batted my eyes heavily to keep my tears at bay.

"You know the guy that I have been telling you all about, Chazman? He's been here a few times and has even spoken to you too. I think you both will be happy to know that he saw something in me and has asked me to be his wife." I chuckled when the wind blew heavily and almost knocked my sunglasses off of my face.

"Calm down, Daddy. I actually think that you would have liked him. He takes good care of me, not just financially, but emotionally and spiritually just how you did for mommy. As a matter of fact, these visits every Saturday was his idea… guys, he's so fucking good to me. He's like my soul whisperer. You know when you're sick, and you have that one special thing that will make you feel better? You know Daddy, like mom's special soup that she would make when one of us are feeling down or having a runny nose? Well Chazman is my special soup.

He can make anything better…"

My voice trailed off and a smile slowly crept upon

my face as I thought about Chaz. He was fucking nuts,

but hell, so was I. I laughed out loud and shook my head.

The wind blew again, and that was when I noticed that

someone had been here. My mother had fresh flowers on

her grave. I looked at the expensive arrangement and

knew exactly who was behind the visit. I looked at my

father's site and saw that there was a small envelope. I

opened it and pulled out the letter that was inside. At this

point, I couldn't control the tears that began to fall.

"Mr. McPherson,

First, I would like to say that it has been a pleasure

talking to you and getting to know more about you and your wife. I would like to compliment the both of you on such a great job the two of you did in raising my queen. She has brought about a new found happiness in me, one that I knew existed but didn't care to show. She has a way of making me aware of feelings that I try to hide, but soon realize that there isn't a point, because she feels the same way. Brailynn is extraordinary, and I pray for the day that she blesses me with a daughter, and I can sit back and watch her become the woman that her mother is today. I want you to know that your baby girl is in good hands. I would stop at nothing to keep her safe, and I would do everything in my power to keep her smiling and happy. She deserves that, and I believe that I deserve her.

I'm writing you because I would like to know if it's okay if I ask Brailynn to marry me. Before you go hunting me and shit, know that I am a good man who means well when it comes to her. I have a son who is eight, and Brailynn plays a major role in his life. He calls her his mom, and she means more to him than the woman who

actually birthed him. The way that your daughter loves my child as

her own makes me want to love her forever and a day, but I need

your acceptance of that. She misses you and your wife terribly, and I

would like to make sure that the two of you remain a part of her life

as well as mine. So, if you're with it, can you send me a sign or

something? I would truly appreciate it.

-Chazman."

I folded the letter back up and wiped my eyes. I was
crying so hard that I had a river of snot flowing from my
nose along with a headache. That man never ceases to
amaze me. I stood to my feet and placed a kiss on each of
my parent's tombstone and stuck the letter in my back
pocket. I then ran full speed to my honey and jumped in
his arms. He caught me just in time and picked me up like

the big baby that I was and held me tightly. He rubbed my back in a soothing manner as I cried my eyes out. When I finally had enough, I lifted my head and gazed into his tight dark brown eyes.

"Thank you. Thank you for thinking of me and including them in one of the most important days of my life. I love you so much, Chazman. Like, I don't even know what to say." I kissed his lips and allowed him to wipe my face free of snot and tears.

"You don't have to say anything or thank me babe. I know how much your parents mean to you. Anything that's important to you is important to me. I will never get to meet your mother and father, but I will be connected to them spiritually." He gave me another tight hug and placed me on my feet. Grabbing his hand, I let him lead the way back to the car. "On the next visit, I'mma need you to talk to your pops about that wind. When I read the letter to him and asked for a sign, the wind blew so hard that it knocked the letter out of my hand. I had to ask him if that was a 'no'," Chaz said, causing the both of us to laugh.

"What did he say?" I asked. I was feeling so good at that moment that I wanted to bottle the feeling and keep it forever.

"I knew that it was a yes when I felt a cool calming breeze. I got daddy's approval; now you're stuck with me forever." Chaz opened the passenger's side car door for me and helped me in. I watched as he made his way to the driver's side door, then I leaned over the console and opened it for him. He slid in and cranked the car up. I grabbed his hand and brought it to my lips, kissing the back of it softly.

"Stuck with you is the best place to be." I told him, meaning every word that came out of my mouth.

~~~~~

"Finally, this bitch has decided to show up!" I heard Chandler when I walked into the room. Today was the day of Breeland and Lil Chaz's party, and we were meeting at the hotel that we were having it at to help set up and make sure that everything was going okay.

Since Bree-Bree didn't have many friends, the first part of the party that started at five was going to be a princess sock hop. Just a little party-like setting where her and her friends dress as their favorite Disney character princess and dance to theme music. We even hired the actual princess that dress up at Disney land to attend.

That was what Lil Bit wanted, so of course, Chand made

sure she had it.

My boy, on the other hand, was growing up, and

when he presented the idea of having a foam party with

swim trunks and girls having bathing suits, I was totally

against it, but of course, he wore me down, and I

eventually gave in. Lil Chaz's party was scheduled to start

at eight tonight and end at eleven. I had to admit that I

was excited for both parties like they were mine. Both of

my babies were growing up. Tomorrow would be

Breeland's actual birthday, and she'd be turning the big

six. The day after that was be Lil Chaz's, and he'd be nine.

Damn, nine years old? Maybe Chazman is right. It is time for us to

have another kid.

"Sorry I was late; I was with my baby." I said, placing my purse on one of the hotel room beds.

"You good, boo; you haven't missed shit. Chand's fat ass ordered room service. We've been eating since we got here." Noni said, with a bowl full of pineapples and strawberries. Looking at all of their food and what was left on the table that they had sat up in the room had my mouth watering. I went to wash my hands so that I could help myself.

"What's all left to do?" I asked no one in particular. I bit into the crispy bacon and almost came. I had skipped breakfast this morning, and my stomach could tell.

"Nothing really; I thought that we would still have to set some things up, but the hotel staff took care of everything. It's three o'clock now. Lil bit is taking a nap, and Lil Chaz is at the barber shop getting his hair cut. We got time to kick it." I nodded my head and continued to eat and rock to the music that the girls had playing in the background.

"Alright hoes. I got some shit to tell y'all." Rori said, taking a sip of her orange juice. We all gave her our undivided attention, ready to hear what tea she had brewed for the day.

"I'm pregnant." she revealed with a small smile. We all jumped up like a fire had been lit under our asses and gathered around her.

"Damn, what water have y'all hoes been drinking?" I asked, realizing that all my girls were pregnant except for me. They all laughed and waved me off, but I was still shocked that they pulled the shit off like this. "Shit, I know if y'all ain't been doing nothing else, y'all been fucking." I laughed at my own joke, and so did they. Of course, they wouldn't take offense. They knew that I didn't have the sense that God had given me. I don't know where that shit went.

"Mommy!" we heard Breeland say. I placed my hand over my mouth, because I forgot that she was in the living room part of the room taking a nap.

"Yeah, baby?" Chand answered back.

"Y'all too loud!" she yelled like she was really pissed that we had woken her up. I started giggling, because Bree was hell when it came to her sleep.

"My bad; go back to sleep!" Chand said and pulled up the door that connected to the bedrooms some more.

"Are y'all ready for that?" I asked the three of them. They all looked at each other waiting on the other to answer until we all busted out laughing.

"Hey, I was just having sex. I didn't know I would get pregnant." Noni said, causing us to stop laughing. I looked at her long and hard waiting on her to realize what she said, but it never registered with her. She got up and fixed herself another plate. See, now I was worried and decided that it was time that I talk to my cousin, because Noni's slowness done went too far. *Does she really not know where babies come from?*

"What you think about the guys planning Lil Chaz's party." Chand asked me, and I couldn't help but to roll my eyes. The girls and I did everything for Breeland's set, and I don't know why, but we decided to let the guys plan Lil Chaz's.

"Don't even get me started. There's no telling how that shit is going to turn out." I said biting into my fruit salad. The shit was so sweet and juicy that a little of the juice dripped down my chin.

"Damn, you have a hole in your lip don't you?" Chand cracked, making the girls laugh. I flipped them off and kept right on eating.

"I bet money that Lil Chaz's party is going to resemble one of a sixteen-year-old's. Y'all know they talk and treat him like he is grown," Rori said, making a point. It was in that moment that I began to regret letting them plan my baby's party.

"Let's just give them the benefit of the doubt. We're not going to speak foolery into existence. Everything is going to be just fine." Noni said. I bowed my head and prayed that she was right.

"I would like to thank everyone who came out to my party and for all the gifts and money that I got. I wanna say thank you, and I love you Mommy and Daddy, because this was the best birthday ever!" Breeland beamed. It was five minutes until Lil Chaz's party was scheduled to start in the room next door. We didn't plan for a six-year-old party to last so long but the kids were having so much fun that we let them tire themselves out. Parents kept telling us that we were doing them a favor, because after a good bath, the kids were sure to go straight sleep. The same held true for Breeland. You could see it in her eyes that she was beyond sleepy.

"Baby girl, I'm going to take Lil bit to the room and lay her down for bed. Y'all go ahead and head on over to Lil Chaz's party. Brailynn, try to keep your head until afterwards." Mama Nae said, kissing us all on the cheek. I wondered what was to her warning me keeping my head but decided to take in stride. One thing was for certain, Mama Nae had never steered me wrong.

"Come on, Ma, y'all ready?" Chaz asked, walking up on me. I just looked at him, seeing if there was anything that I could detect. When I didn't see anything, I allowed him to pull me away.

"WHAT THE HELL!?" I heard someone say, but I was in so much shock that I couldn't determine who it was. Right when we walked into the room, it was the likes of a club scene. The lights were dimmed, and the tables were placed scattered like a lounge area with colorful strobe lights bouncing everywhere and the music was blaring. On the far right wall was a picture booth, and on the left wall was the food bar. Walking further into the room, we came up on the dance floor that you could barely see the people dancing due to the black light that overshadowed it, however enough light was shown that I could see that the girls here were dressed in little ass two-piece swimming suits, and the boys in swimming trunks. Around their necks were glow sticks, and they all looked to be having the time of their life. But fuck that! This is a nine-year old's party; Lil Chaz was not some college kid. Foam and water were everywhere.

I bent down to take off my shoes, and when I came back up, I turned around and clucked Chaz's foolish ass with my Jordan.

"Seriously, Chazman! This is what you plan for your nine-year-old son? A foam party doesn't call for all of this! Where the fucking lights at? Cut that shit on!" I fumed, straining my eyes to find a light switch.

"Chill Kironda, you mad at the wrong person. I thought Lil Chaz was old enough so I let him plan his own party. I just paid for everything. And you need to quit it with that "your" shit, because he ain't just my son. He's yours too!" Chaz said, looking down at me with a hard glare. I wanted to get in his ass some more about allowing Lil Chaz to even plan his own party, but the look

in his eyes had me deciding against it.

"Where is he?" I asked searching the room again.

"Here he comes now." Chaz said, and as if on cue,

the DJ began to speak.

"The man of the night is in the building! Y'all give a

big round of applause for the flyest nine-year-old to ever

do it! Duke Chazman! We see you boy; this is his special

request for all the ladies and all the girls to the dance

floor, let's go!"

See girl, I know that you're a freak, you sliding down that

pole

The way she looking at me, I'm giving up the dough

So won't you put the pussy on me, yea girl I said won't you put that pussy on me

I sat back in horror as I watched my son with his bare bird chest out, Versace swim trunks, and slides on his feet. With blacked out Aviator Ray Ban sunglasses on his face, and multiple gold chains around his neck, he walked off the stage next to the DJ like he was the shit. He went up to a little ass hoochie mama that looked to be years older than my baby, then I watched as he first slapped her on the ass and then bent her over as she twerked on him like his parents weren't here supervising.

"Do you see this shit?" Rori asked me. I couldn't answer. I was so fucking pissed that my entire body began to shake. Before I knew it, my feet were moving in his direction. When I was in arm's length of him, I snatched

Lil Chaz up so hard that it made the girl that was dancing on him fall dead on her face. *Good for you, heffa!*

"Mom!" he said, trying to help her up, but I wasn't hearing it!

"Don't *Mom* me!" I yelled, causing a few of his friends to look our way.

"Babe, let him make it. As bad as I want to get in his ass, we can't do it right now without embarrassing him on his birthday. As soon as we get to the room, we can handle him. Not now, though." Chaz whispered in my ear. I was so pissed that my teeth began to chatter in my mouth.

"I'm sorry, Ma. I'll be more mindful." Lil Chaz said hugging me. I calmed a little but was still pissed the fuck off.

"This isn't over." I said to him before walking away with the girls and Chaz following behind.

An hour or two had passed, and I had just calmed down enough to enjoy the party from the corner the girls and I were seated at. We had just gotten off of the dance floor from trying to battle these young girls who thought that they could out dance us, but of course, we showed them up. I was fanning myself with one hand and sipping on my pineapple peach margarita that I had gotten from the bar that was for the parents when I heard a lot of commotion going on from the front of the entrance. There was a crowd surrounding the area so I couldn't see what was going on. Thinking that it was a couple of the kids, I got out of my seat and headed that way.

"Get this broad the fuck away from round here before shit gets serious!" I heard Chazman say. That was enough for me to bombard my way through the crowd to see who it was that had my man so heated. When I made it to the front, I came face to face with the last person I expected to see.

"What's the matter? Cat got your tongue?" she smirked at me like her presence really meant something. Little did she know, I would get it poppin any time, any place. If this was what she wanted, then I was about to deliver.

"What the fuck is this bitch doing here?" Chand asked, coming to stand right beside me.

"I know how y'all like to jump, so I brought someone along with me." she said, smiling, like I was phased. When she brought in her help, I couldn't help but to laugh.

"Man Brailynn, get that bitch!" I heard Henny say. And that was all she wrote.

TO BE CONTINUED...

SUBMISSION GUIDELINES

Silver Dynasty Publications is currently accepting submission for the following genres:

Urban Fiction

Street Literature

Women's Fiction

African American Romance

Multicultural Romance

Erotica

Send the first 3 chapters of your manuscript, a synopsis, and contact information to silverdynastypublications@yahoo.com for consideration.